A KISS AND A PROMISE

Just as Autumn Daniels is getting her life back together after her husband's death, Matt Kingston returns. He'd left her five years ago with a kiss and a promise he never kept. Then, pregnant and alone, she'd turned to his brother — however, his proposal of marriage was just an elaborate scheme of vengeance. But now, as Matt melts the ice around her heart, is it Autumn he wants — or his daughter? This time, is his promise of love forever?

Books by Moyra Tarling
in the Linford Romance Library:

A TENDER TRAIL

MOYRA TARLING

A KISS AND
A PROMISE

Complete and Unabridged

LINFORD
Leicester

First published in 1989
in the United States of America

First Linford Edition
published 2010

British Library CIP Data

Tarling, Moyra.
  A kiss and a promise. - -
(Linford romance library)
1. Widows- -Fiction. 2. Single mothers- -
Fiction. 3. Love stories. 4. Large type books.
I. Title II. Series
823.9'2–dc22

ISBN 978–1–44480–417–1

Published by
F. A. Thorpe (Publishing)
Anstey, Leicestershire

Set by Words & Graphics Ltd.
Anstey, Leicestershire
Printed and bound in Great Britain by
T. J. International Ltd., Padstow, Cornwall

This book is printed on acid-free paper

My thanks to all
the 'Ladies of the Club'

1

Autumn Daniels curled her fingers around the telegram in her hand and tried to quell the feeling of panic threatening to take hold.

Will be there for the opening. Arriving Friday.

Matt

Though she'd known Matt had been issued an invitation to the opening of the new wing of the Wheeler Gallery, and the first exhibition of Paul's last series of paintings, she'd never expected for a moment that he'd come.

She began to pace the small area of her bedroom wishing now she'd refused the chairman's invitation to cut the ribbon at the official ceremony. But, as Paul's widow, she'd really had no choice in the matter.

Why had Matt decided to come? He'd been touring Europe with the Canadian Ice Hockey Team for the past eight months, and as a result of a car accident on one of Germany's speedy motorways, he'd been in a hospital recovering from a broken leg when he'd learned of Paul's death. He'd missed the funeral, a circumstance Autumn had, at the time, been grateful for.

But he was coming today. The piece of paper in her hand gave testimony of that fact, and the thought brought the panic bubbling to the surface once more.

She'd always known that someday she'd have to tell Matt the truth about Paul's illness, but now that the day appeared to be at hand, she shied away from it. Only a select few had known that Paul had died fighting a rare form of leukemia. Matt had not been one of them.

Now Matt's arrival and the questions he was bound to ask threatened to destroy the peace and contentment she'd only recently begun to know.

During the past six months, since Paul's death, she'd made a start at rebuilding a life for herself and her four-year-old daughter, Holly. And tonight she would fulfill her last obligation to the man who had manipulated and used her, the man who'd been her husband.

'There you are!' Autumn's bedroom door opened and Holly came running in.

Autumn hurriedly blinked the tears from her eyes and crumpled the telegram in her hand as she turned to smile at the bundle of energy that was her daughter. 'Were you looking for me?'

'Yes,' came the reply as Holly jumped onto her mother's bed and turned to face her. 'I want to come with you tonight. Please! Can I come?'

Autumn leaned over to kiss the child's blond head. 'I'm sorry, darling, but I'm afraid tonight is for grown-ups only.'

'But I want to see Daddy's painting of me,' Holly said, the trace of a whine in her voice.

Autumn lifted her daughter from the bed and set her on the floor. 'Darling, we've been through this before. You know Daddy didn't paint pictures of people.'

'But he promised me he'd paint my picture,' Holly insisted.

Autumn tried to keep the note of exasperation from her voice. 'I'm afraid Daddy didn't always manage to keep his promises,' she said evenly, annoyed that she was covering for Paul, even now. 'I'll take you to the gallery one day soon and you can see for yourself.' She clasped the small hand in hers. 'Let's go downstairs. I think I smell popcorn. Mrs. Brady said she'd make you some.'

'Popcorn!' Holly squealed, and tugging her hand free, she raced off.

Autumn smiled and followed at a slower pace. As she descended the stairs, her thoughts turned to the evening ahead.

This showing of Paul's paintings had generated a great deal of excitement, understandably so, for since his death his landscapes had been very much in demand. Tonight promised to be a gala occasion, and she'd actually been looking forward to an evening out. Until the telegram from Matt had arrived . . .

Her heart skipped a beat as he drifted into her thoughts once more, and she tried to tell herself it was fear, and not excitement, that was responsible for her reaction.

When she entered the kitchen a few moments later, Autumn found Holly helping herself to a handful of popcorn from the large bowl in the middle of the table.

'Where's Mrs. Brady?' Autumn asked, glancing around the kitchen for the house-keeper she'd hired shortly after Holly's birth.

'She went downstairs to the freezer to get the ice cream,' Holly said through a mouthful of popcorn.

5

'Holly, don't speak with your — 'The chime of the doorbell suddenly echoed throughout the house, and Autumn froze.

'I'll get it! I'll get it!' Holly chanted, and before Autumn could stop her, she pushed the kitchen door open and was gone.

She knew she shouldn't let Holly answer the door alone, but she felt as though her feet were glued to the floor. Holding her breath, she strained to catch the sound of a man's voice — Matt's voice — but all she heard was Holly's greeting. Annoyed at her own foolishness, she forced herself to move. She was halfway to the kitchen door when Holly came bursting in.

'Mummy, there's a man at the door. He says he's my Uncle Matt. Come and see.'

Autumn felt the blood drain from her face as she bent to grasp the child dancing at her feet. She hugged Holly to her and closed her eyes, willing her heart to stop its frantic pounding. As a result, she neither heard nor saw the kitchen door swing open.

'Hello, Autumn.' A deep, familiar voice filled the room, sending uncontrollable shivers of awareness across her skin. She opened her eyes and over the child's shoulder saw Paul's stepbrother, Matt, dressed in blue jeans and a red pullover sweater, standing in the doorway. Autumn's hold on Holly tightened as she met his gaze, and she tried to ignore the traitorous leap of her pulse at the sight of him.

'Mom, you're squishing me.' Holly's plaintive cry broke through to her and reluctantly Autumn released the child and slowly stood up.

'Hello, Matt. How are you?' she asked, relieved that her voice sounded normal. As her glance slid over him, all her senses seemed to cry out in silent recognition, and she found herself thinking that he was still by far the most attractive man she'd ever known.

'I'm fine,' he lied. In actuality his knee was throbbing painfully, and the headache he'd been fighting from the moment the plane had touched down an hour ago was growing steadily worse.

'I was surprised when I got your telegram,' she said. 'I thought you were staying in Europe.'

'I changed my plans,' Matt replied, but before he could say more Holly intervened.

'Are you really my uncle?' Her question startled them both, and Matt dropped his gaze to stare at the blue-eyed child regarding him earnestly.

'Yes, I am,' Matt said as the ghost of a smile curled his mouth.

'Then how come you've never been to our house before?' she asked.

'Oh, but you're wrong. I have been here before,' he countered.

'You have?' Holly kept her gaze on Matt, her expression suggesting she was not at all convinced.

'Yes, I have,' he assured her. 'You were only a few months old at the time and, as I recall, you were fast asleep in your crib,' Matt told her before glancing back at Autumn. The resemblance between them was unmistakable. The child was going to be as beautiful as her mother.

And Autumn was beautiful. The pale green blouse and matching slacks she wore accentuated her porcelain skin and outlined a figure that was close to perfection. Her shoulder-length blond hair, two shades darker than Holly's, framed a face that was almost classic in its elegance.

It was a face that had haunted him over the years. He'd never been able to forget those exquisite features, nor the intoxicating mixture of innocence and fragility she possessed. But now her blue eyes held a look of pain and sorrow as well as a quiet maturity he'd never seen before.

'I remember,' Holly was saying as she crossed the room toward him. 'You play hockey. Daddy watched it on TV sometimes, but he didn't like it much.'

At the child's casual mention of Paul, Autumn saw Matt's jaw tighten and the expression in his eyes grow bleak. She could see instantly that his pain and grief were still very close to the surface, and her heart filled with compassion.

'Have you come to look after us?' Holly asked. 'Mummy says everyone should have someone to look after them. Mummy looked after Daddy for a long — '

'Holly!' Autumn quickly cut in, stopping the child's runaway tongue. Her heart was racing as she continued. 'Why don't you see if Mrs. Brady needs help with the ice cream?' she asked, all the while silently praying Matt wouldn't ask Holly to finish what she'd been saying.

When the door closed behind Holly, Autumn let out a silent sigh of relief.

'She's a beautiful child,' Matt said softly. The sincerity in his voice caught Autumn completely off guard, and it was several seconds before she could speak.

'Thank you,' she said, carefully avoiding his eyes, fearful he would see her reaction and guess the reason for it. She was being foolish, of course. He had never asked, never even suspected. Why should he? Paul had gone to great lengths to keep the truth from the step-brother he'd secretly despised.

He'd been an expert at hiding his true feelings. But Autumn had only been married to Paul a short time before she discovered the real man.

A shiver chased down her spine, and resolutely Autumn thrust the memory aside. Paul no longer had the power to hurt her. She was free; the charade was over. But there was one thing she had to do. And she might as well get it over with.

'Matt, there's something I have to . . . ' she began, but he forestalled her.

'There's so much I want to say, to ask. But right now all I really want to do is lie down for a while.' He touched a hand to his forehead. 'It was a long flight and I'm bushed. I should have checked into a hotel first, then called.'

He turned toward the door.

'You can rest in the guest room if you like,' she suggested. 'The opening isn't until seven,' she added, then wondered at her own wisdom in making the offer. But he did look tired, she thought; in fact, the pallor of his face suggested more than tiredness. 'Are you feeling all right?'

He turned, and at the sudden movement, pain shot through his knee. He made a grab for the nearby counter.

'What's wrong?' Autumn was immediately at his side, grasping his arm and holding him steady.

'I think I'd better sit down,' Matt said, his breathing uneven.

Autumn put her arm around his waist and helped him to the nearest chair.

'Damn!' Matt muttered the curse into her ear as she slowly lowered him into the chair. She felt the warmth of his breath fanning her face, and her eyes lifted to meet his for a brief but heart-stopping second. She dropped her lashes and quickly drew away, but clinging to her now was the fragrance of lime and leather as well as the more earthy scent of his masculinity. A warmth invaded her cheeks and her heart was tripping over itself to catch up with the beats it had missed. She drew a steadying breath, annoyed at her reaction and relieved that Matt seemed not to have noticed.

His head was bent, his breathing shallow and his face deathly pale.

'You look awful,' Autumn said.

Matt raised his head and managed a rueful smile. 'Thanks.'

'What's wrong? Are you ill?' She took a step back wanting to put as much distance between them as she could.

'It's my knee,' he told her as he gently massaged the joint in question. 'I injured it in an exhibition game a month ago. Someone checked me from behind and sent me flying into the boards, knee first.'

Autumn shuddered, her imagination providing her with a vivid picture.

'It was showing no signs of improvement, so the team doctor thought I'd better . . . ' But Matt didn't get to finish, because the kitchen door opened and they were joined by Holly and the housekeeper.

'Mrs. Brady couldn't find any ice cream,' Holly said mournfully. 'We took everything out and looked everywhere. It's cold down there,' she added with a pout.

'I'm sorry, Mrs. Daniels — ' Caroline Brady began, then stopped when she saw Matt.

Autumn smiled at the older woman. 'You remember my husband's step-brother, Matt Kingston,' she said.

'Yes, indeed,' Caroline said, nodding to Matt.

'Mrs. Brady,' Matt acknowledged.

'Matt's here for the opening tonight,' Autumn explained.

'Are you going to stay with us?' Holly asked, moving to stand by Matt's chair.

Matt found it difficult not to smile. Holly's blue eyes regarded his, eagerly awaiting a reply. He glanced at Autumn and caught a look in her eyes he couldn't quite define. 'Actually, I haven't thought much about where I'll stay.'

'You can stay with us. Can't he, Mummy? We have lots of room,' Holly stated matter-of-factly.

'He's certainly welcome . . . ' Autumn began, wishing not for the first time that Holly wasn't such an outgoing and talkative child.

'If you stay here, you could come and see me at my skating class tomorrow.' Holly turned back to Matt and regarded him hopefully.

'I didn't know you could skate,' he said with a smile.

'I'm going to be an ice dancer when I grow up,' Holly informed him, her face shining with pride.

'I'd love to stay, and I'd love to come and watch you skate,' Matt assured her, and was immediately rewarded by a brilliant smile from the little girl.

Watching the exchange, Autumn

suddenly found herself fighting to hold back the tears stinging her eyes. She swallowed, trying to rid herself of the emotion clogging her throat, relieved Matt was too preoccupied with Holly to notice.

'Caroline.' Autumn's voice sounded husky. 'Perhaps you could take Matt's luggage to the guest room.'

'Thanks, Autumn,' Matt said as he carefully eased himself out of the chair. The pain had subsided and was now the insistent ache he'd been living with for the past month. As he followed Caroline Brady from the kitchen, he tried to minimize his limp. The team doctor and the coach had been right — something would have to be done.

'I'll show you the way,' Holly piped up, and scampered after them, leaving Autumn alone with her thoughts.

Matt was staying. But for how long? she wondered. Having him living under the same roof was not a situation she was at all comfortable with. During those brief moments when she'd helped him to the chair, she'd been more aware of him than she cared to admit.

Old, forgotten feelings, emotions and memories she'd banished to the darkest corner of her heart were suddenly struggling to be free. But there was no going back, even if she wanted to. Angrily she blinked away the tears threatening to fall.

She only had herself to blame. She'd been a fool to have thought herself in love with Matt in the first place. Long ago she'd trusted him, thought he cared for her. But he'd disappeared from her life as if he'd been a dream, leaving her lost and afraid and vulnerable.

But she'd been an even bigger fool to have been taken in so completely by Paul. He'd seen her vulnerability, her desperation, and he'd deliberately taken advantage of the fact that she'd had no one else to turn to.

She'd gone from the frying pan into the fire, and the error in judgment she'd made had changed her life irrevocably. But she'd learned her lesson, and learned it well. Never again would she give her trust so blindly, so completely, to anyone.

She had everything she needed for a full and happy life: a beautiful daughter, a lovely home, a few good friends and her nursing career. After Holly's birth she'd insisted on returning to nursing school in order to complete her degree. It was a decision she'd never regretted, for without her degree she would never have been able to get the part-time job at the clinic where she'd been working for the past four months. Not that she needed the money. Paul had fulfilled at least one promise — to provide for Holly.

Nothing was more important to her than her daughter. And now there was just the two of them. It was enough. It had to be.

★ ★ ★

'Mummy! The taxi's here.' Holly was calling from the foot of the stairs, and

18

as Autumn descended, she tried to ignore the ripple of apprehension she felt at the sight of Matt standing beside her daughter.

He looked incredibly handsome in a black tuxedo with a white ruffled shirt and black bow tie. Her heart started to dance crazily in her breast, and she had to grip the banister tightly in order not to miss a step.

Matt couldn't take his eyes off Autumn. She looked stunning in a sleeveless black dress, cinched at the waist with a wide silver belt and decorated at the throat with a silver filigree brooch in the shape of a butterfly. Her hair was pulled back from her face and coiled into an elegant chignon at the nape of her neck. The earrings she wore matched the brooch at her throat.

His mouth went dry as he watched her descend, and somewhere deep inside him a locked-away memory stirred and a door that had been firmly closed for years inched open a crack.

Not for the first time he found himself wondering at the feelings she could so easily arouse within him. He'd dated her first, that summer so long ago. But she'd married Paul . . .

Thoughts of his brother suddenly filled his mind, and instantly he was swamped with feelings of both sadness and guilt.

'You look pretty, Mummy,' Holly said when Autumn reached them.

'Thank you, darling,' Autumn said, and accepted the silver clutch purse her daughter handed her.

Autumn held her breath as she slid her arms into the coat Matt was holding for her. She managed to avoid touching him and turned quickly to kiss Holly. 'We won't be late. And I promise to come in and kiss you before I go to bed,' she added before Holly could voice the request.

'You can come in and kiss me good-night, too, Uncle Matt,' Holly said, giving him the full benefit of her innocent blue eyes.

The look Holly bestowed on him warmed Matt's heart and lifted his sadness a little. 'I'll do that, pumpkin,' he said, and with a finger he gently tapped her on the nose.

'Have a good time,' said Mrs. Brady as the door closed behind them.

Once seated in the taxi, Autumn busied herself locating the seat belt and tried not to think of the man next to her. When her leg accidentally brushed his, she was unprepared for the rush of heat that suffused her face at the contact.

'Wheeler Gallery, please,' she said a little breathlessly, and sank back against the upholstery, trying to uncoil the knot of tension tightening within her, fighting against unseen forces that seemed so highly tuned to Matt's presence. But sitting next to him, their bodies almost touching, was sending shivers of warning across her skin.

Her fingers curled convulsively around the soft contours of her purse as she tried to focus her thoughts on the evening ahead. But as the silence stretched between them, she stole a nervous glance in Matt's direction.

His eyes were closed and she noticed now that he looked slightly more rested than when he'd arrived. Several times throughout the afternoon she'd stopped outside the door of the guest room, her hand poised to knock. Her intention had been to explain to Matt the true circumstances of Paul's death. But each time her courage failed her.

She'd sent Caroline to tell him dinner was ready, then had been guiltily relieved when he'd decided to skip the meal. She guessed that rest was more important to him.

Her gaze lingered on him now, studying his finely chiseled features, taking in the smooth, powerful line of his jaw, the prominent cheekbones, the dark curling lashes and arched eyebrows that hid eyes as blue as sapphires and equally unforgettable. His nose was straight and noble, his lips full and invitingly sensual.

His hair, a rich chocolate-brown color, was long but not unruly. Several strands had fallen forward onto his forehead, and suddenly her fingers itched to comb them back into place.

His eyes fluttered open, and for the space of a heartbeat their gazes locked. She felt suspended in time, trapped in the shimmering heat of his eyes, and in that dark, forbidden corner of her heart there stirred a long-forgotten emotion.

A smile slowly transformed his face, making it impossible for her to even think about breathing. Dear God! Why did he have to be so attractive?

'I'm afraid I'm not very good company tonight,' Matt said. 'I did sleep a little, but I'm not sure it helped.'

'You . . . ' She blinked, cleared her throat and tried again. 'You look better. How's your knee?'

'Damn sore,' he told her, then followed his words with a grin.

'Are you sure you're up to this?' she asked, then immediately wished she hadn't spoken as the smile disappeared from his face and his eyes darkened.

'I'm sure,' he told her. He turned to gaze out at the passing traffic, and when he continued his voice was tight with well-controlled emotion. 'I thought perhaps you'd understand why I want to be there ... need to be there tonight.' He continued to stare through the window, though she felt sure he saw nothing. 'I still can't believe he's gone.' The words were spoken in a harsh whisper of emotion.

'Matt ... ' Autumn reached out to him, hearing the pain and sadness in his voice. He'd been unable to attend Paul's funeral, and it was obvious, at least to her, that Matt was looking for a way to come to terms with his loss.

Tonight, as the city of Vancouver paid tribute to Paul and his work, Matt would, in effect, be saying his own private farewell. And while some people might consider this approach a little out of the ordinary, as a nurse she understood his need to accept his brother's death. She couldn't bring herself to add to his grief, not now. The truth would have to wait.

All the same, she couldn't stop the flash of resentment that came over her when she thought of Paul. Like the cancer that had taken control of his body, hate and jealousy had consumed his mind, until only the shell of the man remained.

She closed her eyes, feeling only compassion and a sense of sadness now. Paul had been a sick man, sick in mind as well as in body, and she hoped that at last he was at peace.

The taxi braked to a halt outside the gallery, shaking Autumn from her reverie. She fumbled in her purse for the fare, but Matt had already beaten her to it. Reaching for the door handle, she quickly stepped onto the sidewalk where a number of curious onlookers had gathered to watch the guests arrive. She waited for Matt to join her and together they made their way toward the huge glass doors leading to the gallery.

As they entered, a man in a black evening suit broke free from a small group of people. His light brown hair glinted in the lights and his hazel eyes glowed warmly as he came forward to greet them.

'Autumn! There you are. I was beginning to worry.' Linc Armstrong kissed Autumn's cheek and took her hand in his in a gesture that was assuredly possessive.

'Hello, Linc,' Autumn said, trying with difficulty to hide her surprise at his unusually affectionate greeting. 'Ah, I'd like you to meet Paul's stepbrother, Matt Kingston. Matt, this is Linc Armstrong. He was Paul's attorney and a dear friend.'

'Of course! The hockey player.' Linc released his hold on her, smiled and extended his hand. 'I thought you were in Europe.'

'Not anymore,' Matt said, and wondered momentarily why he suddenly had the urge to put his fist into the smiling face of the man before him.

Autumn could almost feel the tension emanating from Matt as he turned back to her. There was no mistaking the look of surprise and suspicion she could see in the shadowed depths of his eyes.

Her face grew warm under his steady gaze. But why should she feel guilty? she asked herself. Linc was her friend, nothing more.

'Let me take your coat, Autumn,' Linc was saying. 'I'll be right back,' he added as he made his way toward the coat check counter.

'Linc's daughter, Jennifer, and Holly are friends,' said Autumn. 'They attend the same preschool,' she went on, annoyed with herself for feeling the need to explain her relationship with Linc.

'And is there a Mrs. Armstrong?' Matt asked.

'Linc's wife died two years ago,' Autumn told him.

'I see,' said Matt, and at his words and the tone, Autumn bristled.

'We'd better go right in, darling,'

Linc said as he rejoined them. 'I told everyone that I'd bring you along the moment you arrived.'

'Yes, of course,' Autumn said, and thankfully turned from Matt, but not before she'd seen his dark eyebrows lift fractionally at Linc's endearment.

Annoyance flickered through her once more. The evening had hardly begun and already she was on the defensive. Tonight she needed to be calm and in control, but as she accepted Linc's arm she was hard-pressed to ignore the feeling of foreboding slowly wrapping itself around her.

2

As Matt followed the two people into the gallery, he found his thoughts lingering on the couple in front of him. Linc Armstrong's interest in Autumn was more than professional, that much was obvious, and Matt discovered that this notion did not sit well with him.

As they wound their way around the gallery, Autumn returned smiles and acknowledgments from some friends and acquaintances she passed on the way, but all the while she was acutely aware of Matt's tall, imposing figure behind her.

An enormous red silk ribbon stretched across the huge ornate doors of the new wing, and as they approached the area that was cordoned off, the muted voices of the guests gradually fell silent. Cameras clicked in rapid succession and flashbulbs illuminated the beautiful mosaic walls of the outer hallway.

Frank Simpson, chairman of the board for the Wheeler Gallery, and easily recognizable with his red hair and trim mustache, came forward to greet them.

'Autumn, my dear, you look stunning as usual.' Frank turned to Matt and shook his hand vigorously. 'It's good to see you, Matt. Why didn't you let me know you were coming?'

'I didn't know myself until yesterday,' Matt explained.

Frank patted Matt's shoulder. 'I'm glad you could make it.' He turned and gestured to the row of chairs near the microphone where several board members and their wives were already seated. 'Please sit down. Everyone's eager to get things started.'

Frank crossed to the microphone and waited until they reached the row of chairs before he addressed the assembly.

'Ladies and gentlemen.' The words resounded through the hallway. 'Tonight we are here to open the new wing of the Wheeler Gallery, and in honor of this occasion we are showing for the first time a series of paintings by an artist this city has only recently come to know and love — Paul Daniels.'

After a pause, Frank continued. 'The six paintings you will see tonight depict our beautiful city of Vancouver and are a testimony to the depth of talent this man possessed. As you all know, Paul Daniels died six months ago, but tonight we pay tribute to a man whose legacy will live on forever, a man who will undoubtedly be remembered as one of Canada's finest landscape artists.'

As Autumn listened to Frank talk about Paul, she felt the old anger and resentment rise up inside her. Paul had been a consummate actor, full of charm and sophistication, playing the part of a compassionate, caring man when in fact anything and everything he'd ever done had been purely in his own interest.

He'd had talent, his paintings proved that beyond a doubt, but the recognition and acclaim he'd longed for and dreamed about had for the most part eluded him. Beneath the pleasant façade he showed to the world was a man consumed with jealousy, obsessed with the fact that his stepbrother, a mere sports jock, was held in such high regard by both the public and the media, while his own superior talent was practically ignored.

Autumn moved restlessly in her chair and tried to concentrate on Frank's words.

'In a moment I will ask Paul's widow, Autumn, to step forward and say a few words before she cuts the ribbon that officially opens this new wing. But first I'd like to introduce to you another guest, a man I'm sure you'll recognize. He's one of Canada's most famous sports figures — Paul's stepbrother, Matthew Kingston.'

Applause broke out around her again, but Autumn's thoughts had jumped ahead to the brief speech she'd carefully prepared, and suddenly she couldn't do it . . . couldn't speak the lies . . .

When she heard Frank say her name, her heart began to pound in panic. Everyone was applauding, every eye was on her, waiting for her to come forward, but for the life of her she couldn't move.

Matt glanced at Autumn seated beside him. He could see the tension on her face and the look of panic in her eyes. Frank's speech had undoubtedly evoked old memories and she was obviously overcome with emotion. Without a second thought he put a hand to her elbow and gently urged her to her feet.

'I can't do this . . . ' Her words, barely more than a whisper, were filled with raw emotion, and Matt found himself responding to the unspoken plea.

'I'll handle it,' he quietly assured her, and together they crossed to where

Frank, looking slightly puzzled, stood waiting.

Through the fabric of her dress Autumn could feel the firm support and latent strength behind Matt's touch, and for the first time since his arrival, she admitted to herself that she was glad he was there.

When they reached the microphone it was Matt who turned to address the crowd.

'Ladies and gentlemen, painting was my brother's life, and it was a dream of his to one day have his work displayed here at the Wheeler Gallery. I know I speak for both Autumn and myself when I say how deeply honored we are to be here tonight . . . ' He glanced at Autumn briefly, and when he continued, his voice was husky with emotion. 'Our only wish is that Paul could have lived to see his dream fulfilled. Thank you.'

For several long seconds a hush lay over the crowd. Matt's words, spoken with sincerity and love, filled Autumn with renewed despair, and as applause broke out around them, she realized that the charade was far from over. For as long as Matt stayed she would have to continue to play the part of a woman grieving for her husband.

With a heavy heart she turned to accept the scissors Frank held out to her. Cameras clicked and flashbulbs exploded as the ribbon fell away and the doors to the new wing slid open. Someone touched her elbow, and she turned to find Linc at her side. But the smile she bestowed on him was one of relief, not pleasure.

For the next ten minutes all that could be heard was the exclamations of delight and murmurings of approval as the guests wandered from painting to painting.

Waiters carrying trays of champagne and canapés drifted throughout the crowd, and when Linc commandeered a glass of champagne for her, she gladly accepted.

As she took a sip of the bubbly liquid

her eyes searched the room, looking for Matt. She had no difficulty locating him. His tall figure stood out amid a group of reporters. From across the room their eyes met, and Autumn felt a jolt of awareness race through her.

She dropped her gaze and forced herself to concentrate on what Linc was saying, but not before she'd seen Matt make a move in their direction.

'Mind if I join you?' Matt's deep voice sent a tremor down her spine.

'Not at all,' Linc said with a smile. 'What do you think of Paul's paintings? Marvelous, aren't they?'

A look of pride crossed Matt's features. 'Indeed they are,' he said, his eyes on Autumn, wondering at the tension he could see in every line of her body.

'What courage!' Linc raised his glass in salute as his glance strayed to the painting hanging nearby. 'To be ill for so long, to know he was dying, and yet still be able to create, not one masterpiece, but six . . . Incredible!'

Autumn's heart had stopped beating. Her eyes flew to Matt. His expression was one of shock and confusion, and as her heart began to kick alarmingly against her ribs, she found herself wishing the floor would open up and swallow her.

What she'd feared from the moment Matt had arrived had happened — the secret was a secret no more.

But she couldn't blame Linc. He'd been one of the few who'd known the true nature of Paul's illness, and he'd assumed, as anyone might, that Matt had also known the truth.

Matt turned to Autumn and stared at her in astonishment. He saw the guilt and regret in her eyes and knew instinctively what Armstrong had just said was nothing more than the truth.

She'd told him that Paul, always prone to illness, had come down with pneumonia. Dangerous, perhaps, but not generally fatal. Paul's condition, however, had deteriorated at an alarming rate and his sudden death had come as a shock to everyone.

That was what he'd been told. And being several thousand miles away at the time — lying in a hospital — that was what he'd believed. He'd had no reason to doubt it. And as he continued to stare at Autumn, he saw immediately in the way that she avoided his gaze that she'd lied. But why?

Anger burned a path through him. With controlled deliberation he reached out and removed the glass from Autumn's hand and gave it to Linc, who gazed uncomprehendingly at him. 'Excuse us for a moment,' Matt said, and without waiting for a reply, grabbed her by the arm and ushered her none too gently toward the nearest exit.

'Matt! You're hurting me.' Autumn's protest landed on deaf ears and moments later she found herself in the empty hallway leading to the new wing.

Matt's grip on her upper arm was suddenly released. She met his glare and flinched at the anger she could see in his eyes.

'I want some answers,' he said, his tone clipped.

'All right.' Her chin lifted fractionally and she met his gaze. She realized now how foolish she'd been in putting off this moment, but it was too late for regrets.

'What was Armstrong talking about?' Matt demanded impatiently. 'What did he mean when he said Paul knew he was dying? You told me he knew nothing, that it all happened too fast.'

Autumn swallowed. 'Linc thought you knew — '

'Knew what?' Matt interrupted, taking a step toward her.

'About Paul's condition,' she said, keeping her tone even, all the while wishing there was some other way. But hadn't there been enough lies?

'Dammit! What condition?' Exasperation was evident in every word.

She steadfastly met his imploring eyes. 'Paul died of leukemia.' Her voice was a harsh whisper, and at the look of incredulity on Matt's face, she felt as though someone was squeezing her heart in a vise. His hands dropped away, and he took several steps back.

Behind them the door through which they'd come burst open and Autumn turned to find Linc standing in the doorway. 'Is everything all right?' he asked, but Autumn ignored the question, immediately turning to the man beside her.

Matt was trying desperately to mask his shock. Why hadn't he been told that Paul was so ill? He began to move slowly, laboriously, as though a thousand pounds of weight was pressing down on him.

Linc crossed to where Autumn stood. 'What's going on? Are you all right?' he asked anxiously.

'Yes, of course,' Autumn said, fighting the urge to go to Matt. His head was bent, his shoulders slumped.

'Frank's looking for you,' Linc told her. 'The press want some more photographs. I came to tell you they're waiting.'

Autumn nodded, and with one last glance at Matt, she reluctantly allowed Linc to lead her away.

Matt heard the door click shut, and even before he turned, he knew he was alone. His jaw clenched and his hands curled into fists at his side.

Now that the initial shock was wearing off, his first impulse was to go after Autumn and demand to know why he hadn't been told about Paul's illness.

His mind crowded with questions. When had Paul been diagnosed? And what possible reason could Autumn have for not telling him? As Paul's brother surely he'd had a right to know?

Matt raked a hand through his hair and massaged the back of his neck where a knot of tension tightened inexorably. Anger was still coming at him in waves, and it took a great deal of effort to control his turbulent emotions.

Several people appeared from the direction of the new wing and eyed him curiously as they passed. He took no notice but simply turned and began to make his way back to the gathering. He needed answers and he intended to get them. Silently he made a vow that before the night was over he would find out why she had lied.

★ ★ ★

Autumn's glance kept straying to the entrance as she waited for the photographers to finish. Had Matt left? she wondered. Now that he knew she'd kept the truth from him, she couldn't really blame him if he never wanted to see her again. But she realized that when he'd had time to think, he'd want to know more.

Her head was pounding fiercely, and she was sure her face would crack from the strain if she had to smile one more time for the photographers. A movement at the doorway caught her eye, and her heart lurched painfully when Matt came into view.

'They're all through, Autumn,' Frank said forcing her to consciously drag her eyes away from Matt, who was scanning the crowd, undoubtedly looking for her. 'I really appreciate you being here tonight,' he continued, then frowned at her. 'Are you feeling all right? You look a little pale.'

'I have a bit of a headache,' she told him. 'Would you think it too rude of me if I was to leave now?'

'We'll be sorry to see you go, my dear,' Frank replied. 'But I quite understand. This has been an emotional evening for everyone, but especially for you,' he said, his tone full of concern.

'Shall I drive you home?' Linc, who was standing nearby offered.

A fleeting glance over Linc's shoulder told her Matt had spotted them and was closing in, his face intense, his expression grim.

'Yes . . . please,' Autumn said. The thought of escape brought an eagerness to her voice, but before they could make a move, Matt was upon them.

'Is this a private party, or can anyone join in?' Matt's tone sounded jovial and friendly, but Autumn easily detected the razor's edge of hostility concealed beneath the words.

'I'm afraid the party appears to be winding down,' Frank said as he stood aside to make room for Matt. 'Autumn has a headache and Linc's going to take her home.'

'There's no need for you to cut your evening short, Linc,' Matt said with a smile that didn't reach his eyes. 'I'll see that Autumn gets home safely. It's the least I can do, especially when she's been kind enough to let me use her guest room while I'm here.'

Autumn's hopes sank at Matt's words. She could see the determined light in his eyes and knew that the confrontation she'd wanted to avoid was imminent.

'I really don't mind . . . ' Linc began, glancing questioningly at Autumn.

She managed to smile reassuringly at Linc. 'Matt's right. Please stay and enjoy the rest of the evening. Call me tomorrow and we'll make arrangements to take the girls on that picnic we promised them,' she added, and was relieved to see his features relax in an answering smile.

'Let's have lunch sometime,' Frank suggested to Matt. 'How long will you be in town?'

'Indefinitely,' came the reply. At Matt's decisive tone, Autumn's eyes flew to meet his. A shiver of apprehension danced across her skin, leaving a cold, unwelcome trail.

'I'll call you tomorrow,' Linc said as he leaned over to kiss her cheek.

'Yes, do that,' Autumn answered absently, all too aware of Matt's hand at her elbow and her own heart tripping over itself in instant response.

An attendant quickly located her coat and then held the door open for them.

Outside, the sky was a mass of twinkling stars and the evening air held the last hint of summer in its warm caress. Matt waved down a taxi, and as Autumn climbed in, she drew several deep breaths in an attempt to prepare herself for what was surely to come.

Matt joined her, and she shrank into her corner, keeping as far away from him as she could. He gave the driver the address and sat back against the seat, jaw clenched, eyes staring straight ahead.

She held her breath, waiting for the anger, the outrage, to pour down on her, but instead she was subjected to a long, withering silence.

He used the silence as a weapon, and she found it far more punishing than recriminations. By the time the car drew up outside the house, her nerves were stretched to the breaking point.

A few precious minutes alone, time to collect her thoughts, to regroup, that was what she needed, she told herself as she hurried toward the front door. She fumbled with the keys and unlocked the door. Once inside, she quickly crossed to the stairs.

'I don't want to have to chase after you, Autumn,' Matt's icy tone brought her to a standstill. 'But believe me, I will.'

Her pulse began to hammer against her throat at the unmistakable threat in his voice.

'Surely I'm entitled to an explanation?' Matt's tone cut through her like a knife. 'Wouldn't you agree? But please spare me the lies. This time I want the truth.'

3

Autumn slowly released the breath trapped in her lungs. She couldn't speak, and so nodded her assent.

Retracing her steps, she moved past him into the living room. Slipping out of her coat along the way, she dropped it and her purse onto an armchair before coming to a halt in front of the large bay window that afforded a view of the city skyline. She stood for several seconds staring out at the night, seeing nothing, drawing what comfort she could from the familiarity of the room.

She could feel Matt's eyes boring into her back, but for the moment she lacked the courage to turn and face him.

'Why didn't you let me know about Paul?' Matt demanded, asking the question that had been churning in his mind throughout the drive home.

Squaring her shoulders, she turned and bravely met his gaze, but when she saw the dark, hostile expression on his face, her mouth went dry.

'Why?' he asked again. The word was a plea she couldn't ignore.

She swallowed the lump that had formed in her throat, and keeping her eyes averted, she walked toward the fireplace. 'When Paul found out he had leukemia — ' she began, trying to keep her tone even, unemotional.

'When did he find out?' Matt cut in.

'Ah . . . some time ago,' she replied evasively.

'What does that mean? Six months, a year — what?' he demanded impatiently.

Her pulse jumped in surprise at his question, and it took every ounce of self-possession to meet his eyes. She could almost feel his anger and frustration, and even though she understood it, somehow that did nothing to diminish the sense of helplessness washing over her. 'It really doesn't matter . . . ' she said at last.

Matt stared at her in disbelief. 'It doesn't matter!' His mouth tightened into a thin line and his eyes darkened to midnight-blue. 'Dammit! He was my brother. Surely I had a right to know!'

He was forcing her to look at him, and unblinkingly she met his gaze, wondering momentarily if he realized just how fragile the wall she was hiding behind was. Inside she was trembling, knowing there was no way she could avoid the words she knew would only hurt him more.

'Paul . . . ' She stopped, but his eyes demanded an answer. She spoke softly, hoping her tone might help to ease the shock. 'Paul made me promise not to tell you.'

Matt flinched as if she'd slapped his face, and Autumn's heart contracted in pain at the hurt and confusion she could now see in the shadowed depths of his eyes.

'I don't understand any of this,' Matt said, running a hand through his hair.

'Why would Paul do that?'

'He had his reasons,' Autumn said softly, feeling suddenly tired.

'What reasons?' The anger was back; it was there in the gruff tone of his voice and the grim set of his mouth.

'Leave it, Matt,' she said wearily. 'Just accept the fact Paul wanted it that way — let that be enough.' There was a note of desperation in her voice now, and foolishly she clung to the hope he would take her advice.

'Dammit! It's not enough!' Matt moved to within a few feet of her. 'The last time I talked to him on the phone was a couple of months before he died and he said nothing — nothing. Why didn't he tell me then? Granted our relationship wasn't the greatest, we had our problems, but if I'd known I could have been here for him . . . helped him somehow . . . done something.'

Autumn sighed in frustration, remembering all too clearly how adamant Paul had been that Matt be kept in the dark. She'd thought at first this reaction was merely a phase, part of the denial stage of his illness, but it wasn't long before she realized his reasons were very different and far more disturbing.

Throughout his long illness she'd had ample time to contemplate and analyze Paul's unusual behavior. For her own peace of mind she'd needed to at least try to understand his actions.

The only explanation that seemed to fit was that on learning of his condition Paul had somehow become unhinged. All the jealously, resentment, anger and hate he'd felt for Matt, that had been festering deep inside him over the years, had suddenly erupted.

But how could she tell Matt the man he was grieving for had felt only jealousy and hate for him? He'd never believe her. Paul had been careful to keep the dark side of his personality well hidden. But living in the same house, seeing him each day, she had soon come to know that side.

She glanced at Matt, but he seemed to have withdrawn inside himself, and she found herself wishing there was something she could do to ease his pain.

'Don't torture yourself, Matt. There was nothing anyone could do. Paul knew that,' she told him, hoping somehow her words would offer comfort. 'He wanted to spare you the pain of watching him die — ' she broke off, annoyed with herself for adding this lie.

Dazedly Matt stared at the woman who had once meant so much to him, but had married his brother. The concern in her pale blue eyes was unmistakable, and for a fleeting second he found himself wanting to believe her. But something was wrong. Some instinct told him there was more — that she was holding something back.

His hands came up to grasp her upper arms, and he drew her to within inches of his face. 'There's something you're not telling me,' he said quietly, his eyes fixed on hers as though trying to see into her soul. 'What are you hiding from me, Autumn?'

Her heart faltered, then galloped off at an unsteady pace. She could feel his breath gently stirring the soft tendrils of hair at her forehead, and to her dismay she suddenly found herself struggling to suppress the quicksilver shiver of response his nearness evoked.

'Nothing . . . nothing,' she said, but her voice trembled and lacked conviction.

'You're lying,' Matt snapped in a harsh whisper. 'You seem to have forgotten that I knew you rather well once — intimately, you might say.'

Autumn's shocked gasp was drowned in the words that followed.

'Your eyes give you away,' he continued relentlessly. 'They always were much too expressive.' He released her abruptly and turned to face the fireplace, resting a hand on the mantel. His action gave Autumn several precious seconds in which to recover from the shock of his words. She clasped her hands together in an attempt to stop them from trembling, but there was little she could do to slow the thunderous beating of her heart.

There was nothing left to say. She turned and made her way quietly toward the door, but before she could leave, he spoke again.

'I know you're hiding something from me, Autumn, and I intend to find out what it is. You deprived me of a chance to make my peace with Paul. How could you be so unfeeling, so cruel?'

Autumn blinked furiously, fighting to stop the tears suddenly stinging her eyes from spilling over. Nothing had prepared her for this verbal onslaught, and it was several seconds before she was able to move.

Anger came to her rescue. Like hot molten lava, it bubbled to the surface, and before she could stop to think she spun around. 'How dare you blame me,' she cried. 'I understand how you must feel, Matt, but that doesn't give you the right to accuse me of being insensitive and uncaring. If anyone deserves those labels, it's you.'

Autumn drew in a deep breath and continued. 'Paul was your stepbrother, but I can count on one hand the number of times during the past five years you paid him a visit. Now that he's gone you feel guilty — don't you?' She stopped and drew another breath. 'Shall I tell you who you're really angry with? You're angry with yourself because you know it was through your own neglect that you didn't even know he was ill. If you'd visited a little more often, you would have seen for yourself there was something wrong. But let me tell you something. It wouldn't have mattered, because Paul ha — ' Autumn clamped a hand to her mouth, cutting off the rest of the word. She closed her eyes, unable to believe what she'd almost said. Dear God, what on earth was she doing?

Her eyes flew open and she stared at Matt. His face was pale and there was now a bleak look in those vibrant blue eyes. Something twisted inside her. She didn't want to feel sorry for him. She didn't want to feel anything for him . . .

'Matt, I'm sorry . . . ' She took a step toward him, but he held up his hands to forestall her.

'I think I'd like to be alone for a while,' he said evenly.

Autumn nodded, and without another word she turned and left the room.

Matt stood staring at the closed door for several seconds. Cursing soundly, he twisted away, then groaned aloud at the pain stabbing at his knee. Sweat beaded on his forehead as he sank into a nearby armchair.

Closing his eyes, he leaned back, and as he waited for the pain to subside, his thoughts turned to Autumn and the words she'd flung at him moments ago.

Every word she'd spoken had been true. Some of the anger he felt was indeed directed at himself. Since learning of Paul's death, he'd been swamped with guilt, and the fact that he hadn't been able to attend the funeral had merely compounded it.

They'd never shared a close relation-ship, and he blamed himself for that. When his father married Paul's mother, Matt had been fifteen and Paul twelve. At his father's urging he'd tried to make friends with his new stepbrother, but quickly found that they had little in common.

Paul had been a delicate, sickly child, spoiled and indulged by his mother who'd been widowed shortly after his birth. He'd had little interest in the hobbies and sports Matt was so adept at, preferring to wander off on his own with his sketch pad and pencil to draw the rugged countryside surrounding their home in Prince George in the interior of British Columbia.

Matt, on the other hand, had been fast making a name for himself locally in the hockey arena, and at fifteen he'd lacked the tolerance and patience to deal with Paul's obvious disdain for both him and the game.

For his father's sake, Matt had pretended a liking for Paul he hadn't really felt. He'd been old enough to realize that most stepfamilies had problems at first and that a period of adjustment would be necessary before things would begin to work themselves out.

As time went on, Matt learned to ignore Paul's resentment and jealousy toward him. At times he found himself wondering if he'd ever really get to know his stepbrother.

During the eight years that followed, Matt's time was spent pursuing his hockey career. When he was taken on by a team on the east coast, he'd been thrilled and excited at the prospect of playing for the National Hockey League. He quickly proved himself more than capable of handling the work and pressure that was part and parcel of the game. Before long he was being regarded as a rising young star by the media.

It was the death of their parents in a car accident that brought about a change in his relationship with Paul. In their grief and sorrow a tentative bond of friendship was formed between them, and for the next two years Matt spent his summer hiatus in Vancouver, living in a house Paul rented.

Autumn had lived next door and had dropped in frequently. Though only a year younger than Paul, she had seemed at that time a schoolgirl, and he hadn't taken much notice of her. But during that second summer he had been stunned to discover the changes in her. She had blossomed into a beautiful woman, completely unaware of her own sensuality. Matt shifted restlessly in the armchair as other memories, memories he'd safely locked away, suddenly began to crowd in on him.

It was useless to deny the fact that he'd been in danger of falling in love with Autumn that hot, airless summer five years ago.

Suddenly images of Autumn lying on the sand, her eyes dazed with passion, her naked body trembling with need beneath his, came instantly to mind. He hadn't meant it to happen. But the moment his mouth touched hers he'd been totally and utterly lost. The power of the memory brought a searing pain to his heart, and the old, familiar feelings of guilt assailed him.

He'd hated himself for giving in to his own selfish desires and detested himself even more when he'd had to tell her he was leaving for Europe later that evening to join the Canadian National Team, which was on tour there.

He'd almost asked her to go with him, but he'd pushed that idea aside. She was just starting out in her career — her life was just beginning. How could he expect her to drop everything and go with him, adjust to a way of life she knew nothing about? Hadn't he been selfish enough?

But once in Europe he'd found himself continually haunted by thoughts of Autumn and what he had done. He'd thought about calling her, then remembered that she'd been in the process of moving out of the hospital residence and into an apartment with a nurse whose address he didn't know.

His days had been packed with practices and games, as well as traveling from town to town, but she was never far from his thoughts. He'd called Paul several times without success. He'd been on the road when he'd finally managed to get through. He'd only had time to ask Paul to pass a message to Autumn, telling her he was sorry and that he'd be in touch with her on his return from Europe.

He'd landed in Toronto shortly before Christmas, and once again he placed a call to Paul, hoping for news of Autumn. But he'd been unprepared for the shock of his brother's disclosure that he and Autumn were married.

Somehow he'd managed to offer his congratulations, but from that moment on his relationship with Paul changed dramatically. It had been February before he could bring himself to pay the newlyweds a visit, but while Paul seemed at first pleased to see him, Matt had quickly become aware of tension in the air.

Not once during the two days he'd stayed with them did he ever find himself alone with Autumn — Paul took great pains to make sure that particular circumstance never occurred.

Autumn had been pregnant at the time, and Matt had put Paul's unusual behavior down to a simple case of overprotectiveness. But there had been times when Matt had glimpsed a look in Paul's eyes he was unable to define.

The only explanation that seemed at all plausible was that Paul believed Matt posed a threat to his marriage, and in truth Matt acknowledged to himself that he still felt a strong attraction for Autumn. There was something about her, something unde-finable that called out to him, and though she was now his brother's wife, he'd never quite been able to get her out of his mind.

He'd paid a second visit when Holly had been only a few months old, but again the tension in the house had been almost palpable. After only one day, he'd cut his stay short, unable to relax or feel comfortable in an atmosphere so rife with undercurrents.

And so he'd chosen to stay away, an action that had cost him dearly. If only he'd known . . . but if Autumn was to be believed, Paul hadn't wanted him to know.

Matt shook his head. It was all immaterial now, but he was convinced she was still holding something back. What was it?

With a tired sigh he rose from the chair and slowly made his way to the door, silently vowing to uncover whatever secret she was hiding.

Pain throbbed at his knee as he headed upstairs, bringing another no less important problem to the forefront of his mind. Not until his appointment at the sports clinic on Monday would he know the full extent of the damage he'd done to his knee.

He'd had his share of injuries over

the years, but instinct together with the quality and quantity of pain he'd been dealing with for the past month told him this injury could well prove a major threat to his career.

It was entirely possible that he might have more time than he'd bargained for to uncover the secret Autumn was hiding.

★ ★ ★

Autumn stood by her bedroom window, watching the night sky, listening for the sound of Matt's footsteps on the carpeted floor outside.

She'd left him over an hour ago, but during that time the house had remained eerily silent. Before coming to her own room, she'd checked on Holly, and before kissing the sleeping child, she'd had to rearrange the bedclothes. Somehow they always seemed to be everywhere but on top of Holly.

She hadn't lingered in Holly's room, afraid Matt might suddenly appear. She'd undressed quickly, but was still too restless, too agitated to even attempt to sleep.

Again and again she went over in her mind the angry words she'd rained on him. She'd stopped herself in time . . . just in time.

She began to pace the room again. There would be little sleep tonight, or any night for that matter, as long as Matt was here. She couldn't afford to take his threat of uncovering the truth lightly, and remembering the look of determination she'd seen on his face, she couldn't stop the tremor that rippled through her.

But Matt couldn't stay forever. He was one of hockey's star players. Surely he would be rejoining his team in Europe soon. This thought sent her hopes rising until she remembered the injury to his knee.

Suddenly those moments in the kitchen, when she'd helped him to the chair, flashed into her mind, and her heart began to beat a rapid tattoo against her breast.

A soft moan escaped her lips, and for a fleeting second she covered her face with her hands as once again the memories he'd stirred within her earlier began to nudge insistently at the edges of her mind.

Damn! She turned from the window and crossed the carpeted floor to the bed, the silk of her nightdress rustling in the silence.

Just when she was beginning to get her life back on track, just when she'd begun to forget the nightmare her marriage had been, Matt arrived to create havoc.

That he'd sensed she was hiding something had shaken her more than she cared to admit. She would have to be strong in the face of his determination. It would be devastating enough for Matt to learn of the hatred his brother felt for him, but more devastating still would be the discovery that she had knowingly conspired with Paul to deprive him of a child that was rightfully his.

4

'Wake up, Mummy!' Holly jumped onto Autumn's bed. 'It's nearly time for my skating lesson.'

'What?' Autumn stifled a yawn as she glanced at the clock on her dressing table. She felt as if she'd only just fallen asleep. She'd spent a restless night twisting and turning as images of Matt drifted in and out of her consciousness. 'Goodness! Look at the time! Why didn't you wake me sooner?' She sat up in bed and began to push the covers aside, but Holly's weight impeded her actions.

'It's my fault. I told her not to.' The answer came not from Holly but from Matt, who was standing in her bedroom doorway.

He looked totally at ease and incredibly handsome, and Autumn felt her heart jump into her throat at the sight of him. He wore gray slacks, a blue sport shirt and a tweed jacket, and under his calm scrutiny she felt a warmth creep over her face. Before she could stop herself, she grabbed for the covers and pulled them up around her chin.

'Uncle Matt said we should let you sleep. We had breakfast together. Scrambled eggs is his favorite, too,' Holly informed her before flashing a smile in Matt's direction.,

'I see,' Autumn murmured, fighting to ignore the tingling sensations spreading through her, caused solely by the presence of the man in the doorway. It was with a concentrated effort that she turned her attention back to Holly. 'If you'll give me a few minutes to get dressed, darling, I'll run you over to the rink.' Her voice sounded throaty and breathless, and she wished she didn't feel quite so defenseless.

'No need to rush,' Matt told her as his glance strayed to her hair, fanned out in riotous disarray on the pillow behind her.

Desire clutched at his insides, taking him by surprise. His fingers suddenly itched to bury themselves in those rich golden tresses, and he clenched his teeth in annoyance. 'I called a cab,' he said, keeping his tone even. 'It should be here any minute. In fact, I think that's it now,' Matt added, relieved to hear the crunch of tires on the gravel outside.

'Will you pick me up after my lesson, Mummy?' Holly asked as she hopped off the bed.

'Yes, of course, but — '

'I'll drop her off at the rink on my way to the gallery,' Matt quickly intervened. 'Unless you have any objections . . . ?'

Reluctantly she met his gaze. 'No, but — '

'That's settled then,' came the reply. 'We'd better not keep the driver waiting,' he added, and held out his hand to Holly, who ran to grasp it.

'Bye, Mummy, don't forget to pick me up,' Holly said as they turned to leave.

'Bye.' The word barely made it past the emotion clogging at Autumn's throat. Her eyes were brimming with tears as she watched the twosome walk hand in hand from the room.

It was obvious by the look she'd seen in Holly's eyes that she'd taken an instant liking to Matt, and Autumn wasn't sure whether or not to be glad about that. Undoubtedly Holly had fallen under the spell of his charm, just as she once had. But never again! The price had been far more than she'd bargained for.

Autumn closed her eyes on a sigh and waited for the tension Matt's presence had generated to ease. It wasn't fair, she told herself dejectedly, that one lazy glance from him could send the blood singing through her veins, awakening long-forgotten responses.

He'd caught her by surprise, that was all, she told herself firmly as she pushed back the covers and crossed to the adjoining bathroom. But once in the shower, she adjusted the temperature, hoping the cool spray would help wash away the lingering heat Matt's gaze had aroused.

*   *   *

'This way, Uncle Matt,' Holly said, running toward the sports complex. After paying the taxi driver, Matt, carrying Holly's skates, walked toward the automatic doors.

The complex was relatively new and housed three ice rinks as well as dressing rooms, a lounge area and a cafeteria.

'I change in there,' Holly informed him, pointing to the dressing room to the right of the entrance.

'Will you manage?' Matt asked, handing over her skates.

'Mummy usually helps me, but when she can't stay, my teacher, Miss Audrey, helps me,' Holly said.

'Which rink do you practice on?' Matt asked.

'Rink number three,' she said, and

turned to go. She'd only taken two steps when she stopped and turned to stare up at him. 'You will stay and watch me, won't you?'

Matt was surprised at the serious expression on the child's face. Her blue eyes reminded him so much of Autumn that he felt his heart turn over. 'I promise,' he said earnestly, sensing that his reassurance was important, then was surprised to see a look of disappointment come into her eyes.

'Do you really promise? Cross your heart and everything?' Holly asked, but before he could answer she'd hurried on. 'Daddy always promised, but he never . . . I mean, sometimes he was too busy.' She came to a halt, her eyes beginning to fill with tears, and it was all Matt could do not to pull her into his arms.

'Cross my heart,' he said softly, and followed his words with the action. Instantly Holly's features changed to a heart-stopping smile before she turned and hurried away.

Matt stared after her for several long seconds, puzzled by the exchange, but before he could ponder more on the matter a group of noisy teenagers entered the complex.

'Hey, guys, look! It's Matt Kingston,' one voice yelled, and in moments Matt was surrounded.

Matt nodded and smiled at the eager faces of the crowd gathered around him, shaking hands with several of the youngsters.

'I can't believe it,' said a voice at his side. 'I'm actually standing next to Matt Kingston.'

'You're the best. I wish I could play like you,' another voice piped up.

'Hey, Coach! Look who's here!' said a stocky figure carrying a goalie stick and swinging a bulky equipment bag.

The group stepped aside to let their coach through, and Matt immediately recognized the older man with thinning hair and laughing eyes. He extended his hand toward him. 'As I live and breathe, it's Stan Kirkwood,' he said grasping the hand and hauling the man into his embrace.

'It's good to see you, too, Matt.' Stan Kirkwood punched Matt's shoulder as they drew apart.

'How long has it been?' Matt asked.

'Too long,' came the reply.

'You sure do get around,' Matt said. 'The last time I saw you was six years ago in Ontario. When did you move out here?'

'Four years ago,' Stan said. 'I like the climate.'

'Keeping busy as always,' Matt observed. 'Looks to me like you have yourself a great bunch of guys here.'

'These kids are the best,' said Stan, and at his words there came shouts of agreement from everyone. 'Okay, you noisy lot,' Stan said above the cacophony and instantly his team quieted. 'We're here to practice, remember? So get dressed and onto the ice. Pronto!'

Amid shuffling and good-natured grumbling the team began to disperse, leaving Matt alone with his old friend.

Stan had been quite a hockey player in his heyday, and one of the game's all-time greats. He'd had to retire because of a back injury, but he'd hated inactivity. He'd spent a number of years touring and promoting the sport, and that was how Matt had met him. But for the past ten years he'd been coaching in the minor leagues, and by all reports doing a tremendous job.

'What brings you to Vancouver?' Stan asked a few minutes later.

'A couple of things, actually,' Matt said, but didn't elaborate.

'I thought perhaps you'd heard I've been looking around for a new coach for my team,' Stan said, nodding toward the young men filing into the locker room. 'Have you thought about coaching when you retire?'

Matt laughed good-humoredly. 'Are you trying to recruit me?'

'Why not?' came the jovial reply.

Just then Matt saw Holly emerge from the dressing room. Her face lit up at the sight of him, and he turned to bid his old friend goodbye. 'It's been great seeing you again,' he said, shaking Stan's hand once more.

'Think about what I said,' Stan muttered and, slapping Matt's arm, he walked off toward the locker room.

Matt crossed to where Holly stood with her teacher at the entrance to the rink. Her smile as he approached was totally endearing and effectively melted another corner of his heart.

He stayed for the half-hour private lesson and felt both pride and pleasure as he watched Holly go through the various exercises. For one so small she was already an accomplished skater, and watching her determined little figure complete each exercise, he couldn't help feeling that she might well have the makings of a great athlete.

When the other children began to arrive for the group lesson that followed, Matt called Holly aside for a few moments. Ignoring the pain in his knee, he crouched beside her. 'You skate beautifully, Holly,' he said sincerely. 'I'm sure you're going to be the best figure skater in the world.'

'Do you really think so, Uncle Matt?' Holly asked rather breathlessly, her cheeks pink with effort and her eyes sparkling with happiness.

'I certainly do,' Matt assured her. 'I wish I could stay longer, but I can't today. Perhaps I can come and watch you another time.'

'Would you?'

'I'd love to,' he replied. 'I'll see you back at the house, later,' he added softly, wondering at the emotions slowly curling themselves around his heart. He started to rise, when to his astonishment, she reached over to put her arms around his neck and kissed his cheek.

Fifteen minutes later, as he walked through the doors of the Wheeler Gallery, Matt was still thinking of Holly and the kiss she had bestowed on him. As he rode the elevator to the office of the assistant curator, he found himself thinking, not for the first time, how much he'd envied Paul.

With a sigh he deliberately turned his thoughts to Lenore Fielding, the woman he'd come to the gallery to see. She'd approached him the previous evening shortly after the opening ceremony. After introducing herself, she'd asked when it would be convenient for him to drop into the gallery offices to collect the painting being held for him.

He'd managed to hide his surprise, then suggested a time to meet the next day. She'd promptly agreed, and before he'd even had a chance to ask what painting she was talking about, a small contingency of the local media had surrounded him. When he'd finally managed to extricate himself from the reporters, the lady in question had been nowhere in sight.

Not until he was eating breakfast with Holly had he remembered the incident and the appointment he'd made.

The elevator stopped, he stepped out

into a brightly lit reception area. A moment later, a door to his right opened and Matt found himself face-to-face with Lenore Fielding.

'Mr. Kingston! I'm so glad you came,' she enthused, shaking his hand. 'Please come in. Last night was so hectic, I wasn't sure you'd remember.'

Matt followed the older woman into a small but comfortable office. 'You mentioned something about a painting,' he said.

'We wrote to your Toronto address, informing you we were holding a painting for you,' she told him.

'I've been in Europe for the past eight months,' he explained.

Lenore smiled. 'That would certainly explain why our letters were never answered. Last night when you were introduced . . . Well, I felt it would be a shame to let the opportunity to talk to you slip by.'

'I quite understand,' Matt replied. 'But I must say I'm rather at a loss. Which painting are you talking about?'

'It's by your stepbrother, Paul Daniels, of course,' she said, eyeing him somewhat strangely. 'When the paintings for his exhibition were delivered to the gallery four months ago, there were seven, not six as we'd expected. Taped to the wrapping of one of the paintings was a note, informing us that it wasn't part of the exhibition. On it were instructions to contact you and ask where and when you wanted it shipped.'

'Where is it now?' he asked, suddenly consumed with curiosity. 'Can I see it?'

'Certainly. It's in storage, but I can easily set it up for you in one of the private viewing rooms down the hall.'

'If it's not too much trouble,' Matt said, finding himself unable to quell the feeling of excitement building inside him.

'I'll be right back,' she said. But Matt wasn't listening; his mind was preoccupied with thoughts of Paul. As the minutes slowly ticked by his anticipation grew. He crossed to the window, his mind filling with questions. Why had Paul left such specific instructions regarding the painting? Why hadn't he simply left it with Autumn? Was there a reason for Paul's action? A message?

'Sorry to have taken so long, Mr. Kingston,' Lenore said suddenly, breaking into Matt's thoughts. 'If you'd like to follow me . . . '

'Thank you.' Matt turned from the window where he'd been standing for the past ten minutes, then followed her down the hall to a room at the end. She stopped and held the door open for him.

'I'll leave you to do the unveiling in private,' she said softly as she stood aside to let him pass.

The door closed behind him and Matt moved into the room toward the large easel. He reached out and pulled up the cloth that was draped over the painting. His heart stopped in midbeat, then galloped on as the silence in the room pressed in on him.

It was a portrait! Matt had never

known Paul to paint anything but landscapes, but on the easel stood the most amazing portrait he had ever seen. While the subjects themselves weren't a surprise, he was stunned by the incredible richness and vitality of the piece.

A younger Holly, a baby a little over a year old, was in her mother's arms, her tiny head tilted back, her cherublike face wreathed in smiles. Somehow Paul had managed to capture the child's restlessness, her eagerness to be off, and Matt could almost swear Holly was actually wriggling.

His gaze shifted to the woman holding the child. Here Paul had caught on canvas Autumn's indefinable beauty. Shimmering blond waves framed her classic features, and the pale blue eyes that looked out at him were brimming with love and laughter. Her mouth was so tantalizingly real that Matt felt the old familiar ache of longing well up inside him.

It was the expression in Autumn's

eyes that Matt found completely arresting. As he gazed transfixed at the woman who had been his brother's wife, his heart contracted with pain.

He had never seen a look of such love, of such joy on her face before, and of its own volition his hand reached out to touch her, as if by doing so the emotion evident in the painting would somehow transfer itself to him.

The canvas felt cold against his fingertips, and a shudder passed through his body as his hand dropped away. But he couldn't bring himself to stop staring. He stood for what seemed an eternity, carefully studying each stoke of the brush, each minute detail of the two people Paul had obviously cared deeply about.

The canvas portrayed a woman who looked completely happy with her life. And that, Matt was certain, was the message Paul had wanted him to see. Though he'd thought he'd managed to keep his feelings for Autumn well hidden, Paul had seen through his subterfuge. By leaving him the painting Paul was merely ensuring that Matt wouldn't forget who was responsible for the look of happiness in Autumn's eyes.

He heard the knock on the door, but ignored it.

'Oh, I'm sorry,' Lenore said from the doorway.

'Was there something you wanted?' Matt asked without turning.

'I wasn't sure you were still here,' Lenore said, coming farther into the room. She paused, and Matt knew she was looking at the portrait. 'It's truly fantastic, isn't it? Almost better than the landscapes downstairs,' she went on as she drew abreast of him.

Unable to look at Autumn now, Matt dragged his gaze to Holly's laughing face, and instantly the chill that had been steadily seeping into his bones, and the pain twisting at his heart, began to ease. He felt a smile tug at the corner of his mouth as he took in the look of mischief, warmth and love that was so much a part of the child.

'Such a beautiful baby,' commented the woman at his side.

'A tiny replica of her mother,' Matt said, his tone wistful.

'Do you really think so?' Lenore flashed him a look of surprise. 'She has her mother's hair coloring, I grant you that, but . . . ' She stopped and glanced at Matt for a long moment before turning back to the portrait. 'I'd say she looks more like you!'

The silence that followed her words was shattered by the sound of footsteps in the hallway and a voice urgently calling for Lenore. 'Excuse me,' she muttered. 'Please stay as long as you wish. Stop by my office before you go,' she added as she hurried from the room.

Matt made no reply as the observation she'd made slowly sank in. He recalled with vivid clarity the night he'd made love to Autumn that summer more than five years ago. He'd never been able to get her out of his mind since, never forgotten the way she'd responded to his touch or how incredible that night had been.

He'd known she was innocent, sensed it in the way she'd trembled whenever he was near. And stupidly he'd thought that a few kisses would appease a little of the hunger she'd so easily aroused in him. But the moment his mouth had touched hers he'd known that kisses would never be enough, as every ounce of willpower he'd possessed had been swept away like a leaf in a hurricane.

A ragged sigh escaped his lips, and his hands curled into tight fists as he fought to contain emotions he usually kept strictly under control. With great deliberation he began to study the portrait, carefully scanning the child's features, searching now for any resemblance to Paul. There was none.

Matt continued to stare into the laughing eyes and realized with a jolt that they were exactly the same color as his own.

His heartbeat thundered in his ears

as his mind began to explore the possibility. Was Holly his child? The question played inside his head like a haunting melody, and as hard as he tried he couldn't remember Paul ever telling him the exact date of Holly's birth.

He cursed as he raked his memory for a clue. Holly had been only a few months old when he'd paid his second and last visit to Vancouver. He made some swift calculations, but the numbers only confused him more.

Was *he* Holly's father? A strange new emotion burst to life within him. He'd never known a feeling like it — the simple wonder of knowing that he had helped to create another human being. To be a father!

Matt found himself remembering his own father and the special love they'd shared. And suddenly he wanted it to be true, needed it to be true.

He had to know! If Autumn had lied about Paul's illness, then she was capable of anything, even withholding the truth about Holly's true parentage.

With a last look at the painting, Matt turned and left the room. He stopped at Lenore Fielding's office only long enough to ask her to keep the painting in storage until she heard from him.

Outside, he hailed a taxi. The journey seemed interminable. The thought uppermost in his mind was the possibility that Holly might be his daughter, his own flesh and blood. The more Matt pondered this, the more convinced he became it was true.

But when the taxi drew up outside the house, he found all kinds of emotions churning inside him. Taking precedence over all else, though, was anger.

5

Autumn jumped when she heard the front door slam. She dropped her keys into her purse and hurried out to the hallway, but the sight of Matt, his jaw tight, his eyes blazing, brought her to a halt.

'What is it?' she demanded, closing the gap between them. 'Is it Holly? Is she all right?' Fear made her heart pound, and it was all she could do to control the panic rising inside her.

'Holly's fine,' Matt informed her, keeping a tight rein on his anger. 'Actually, I've just come from the gallery. Did you know Paul left me a painting?'

'What?' Autumn stared in genuine surprise, her concern for Holly momentarily forgotten.

'He left me a painting,' Matt repeated. 'A portrait of you and Holly,' he continued, his eyes watchful.

'But that's impossible,' Autumn said. 'Paul never painted portraits . . . ' Her words trailed off as she suddenly remembered Holly's insistent voice the night before asking to go the gallery to see Daddy's painting of her.

'Lying again, Autumn?' Matt's silky tone sent a shiver of apprehension across her skin, and she closed her eyes, desperately trying to think. Paul had been fanatical at times about his work, and he'd forbidden her to interrupt him while he was in his studio. He could indeed have painted a portrait — but why?

She opened her eyes now and found Matt standing directly in front of her, watching, waiting, and at the look of anger still glittering in his eyes, her heart began to thud in alarm against her rib cage.

'I'm not lying,' she said, but her tone lacked conviction.

'And there's another question I want a truthful answer to — I stress *truthful*,'

Matt said, the hint of a threat in his voice now. 'Is Holly my daughter?'

Autumn gasped, staring at Matt in total shock. Her purse slid from nerveless fingers and skittered to the floor as a wave of nausea swept over her. She felt as if she were standing on the edge of a precipice and one puff of air would send her falling into oblivion.

'Answer me, dammit!' Matt grabbed her by the shoulders as if to shake the answer out of her. 'Is Holly mine? I want the truth. I have a right to know.'

Words of denial almost made it to her lips, but as she stared into his eyes she found she couldn't lie. She wrenched herself free, and on limbs that were anything but steady, she turned and walked back into the living room.

Her thoughts were in chaos, her mind frantically searching for a way out. She knew he was behind her, but she kept her back to him as she struggled for control.

She'd often wondered if Matt had

ever suspected Holly might be his. She'd replayed numerous scenarios in which he'd confronted her, but the reality itself was a far cry from any scene she'd ever imagined.

She drew a ragged breath, fighting with her heart and her conscience. What on earth had prompted him to ask? she wondered. Then the answer occurred to her. The portrait, of course! It had to be. Something in the painting had set the wheels in motion.

Seconds ticked by, and the longer she waited the more menacing his presence became. Even if Matt knew the truth now, she rationalized, nothing he could do or say would change anything. He couldn't take Holly from her . . . for in the eyes of the law she was legally Paul's daughter.

She turned to face him. The rigid stance of his body, the harsh expression on his face and the fury still simmering in his eyes told her that he was only just managing to keep himself in check.

She swallowed. 'Yes. Holly is your

daughter,' she said at last, her voice little more than a hoarse whisper.

Air hissed from between his teeth and his legs suddenly felt weak. It was the answer he'd been hoping for, praying for, but still the knowledge stunned him. For a brief moment he allowed himself to experience the joy that rocketed through him, but the anger racing through his veins quickly drowned the pleasure.

With a mixture of fascination and fear, Autumn watched as Matt's pupils dilated and darkened until they were as black as coal. For a moment she thought she saw a flash of joy, even excitement, in their shining depths, but it was gone as quickly as it came.

'You deprived me of my right to know I had a daughter. Why didn't you let me know?' The words sliced through the air and seemed to carry a multitude of emotions — pain, anguish, bewilderment and, of course, anger.

Autumn opened her mouth to speak, but her throat was paralyzed with emotion and refused to let the words through.

'What about Paul?' Matt continued. 'Where does he fit into this? Were you sleeping with him, too? Did you tell him the baby was his? Is that why he married you?'

Matt was only inches away now. The look of disgust she could see in his eyes made her flinch. Bravely she met his gaze.

'Paul married me because he . . . ' She faltered, and her eyes dropped away from his. How could she tell Matt that the true reason for Paul's actions had been jealousy and hatred? And that by clever manipulation he'd ensured himself that Matt would be deprived of both the knowledge he had fathered a child, as well as the child itself.

'Because he was besotted — no, obsessed with you,' Matt finished for her. 'You had him wrapped around your little finger.'

'No! That's not true,' Autumn burst out, feeling totally sick at heart at his accusations.

'Don't try to deny it. I saw it with my own eyes those few times I was here after you were married. You had him so tied in knots that he even thought I was a threat. Now it all makes sense,' he added, as if to himself.

'Sense!' Autumn repeated the word in a tone that brought Matt's eyes back to her. 'You don't know the half of it,' she said, fighting the anger and despair rising up inside her. 'But there is one thing I will say,' Autumn continued with a calmness she was far from feeling. 'After that night you virtually disappeared, you gave me the distinct impression that what happened between us meant absolutely nothing to you.' Her voice wavered fractionally, but she hurried on, afraid her courage would evaporate. 'I may have been naive enough to let you seduce me, but the blame isn't entirely mine. All you left me with was a kiss and a promise — a promise you never fulfilled. I didn't deprive you of your daughter, Matt. You deprived yourself.' With those words ringing in the air, Autumn pushed past him and left the room.

Her hands shook uncontrollably as she tried to fit the key into her car's ignition. Dear God, why had she told him the truth about Holly? A sob escaped, and for a moment she let her head rest against the steering wheel. But the thought that Matt might come after her had her fumbling with the keys once more.

She remembered little of the journey to the ice rink, and only the fact that she had driven the route numerous times enabled her to arrive safely. She was still trembling when she came to a halt in front of the building.

She hurried inside and instantly spotted Holly sitting with a small group of children. 'Hi, darling. Sorry I'm a little late,' she said as she approached.

Normally Holly raced to greet her, eager to tell Autumn all about her lesson, but today there was no boisterous welcome.

Autumn said nothing until they were

seated in the car. 'What's wrong, darling? Did you have a bad session today?' she asked softly.

Instantly the child's lower lip began to quiver and her eyes filled with tears. 'Miss Audrey told us there's going to be a special concert in two weeks just for dads, cause lots of times they don't get to see their kids skate. But Sally Grant said I can't go, 'cause I don't have a daddy.' Two fat tears rolled down Holly's cheek. 'I can go, can't I?' Blue eyes, so like Matt's, studied Autumn anxiously, and her heart contracted with pain.

'Of course you can, darling,' Autumn reassured her. 'I'm sure Miss Audrey knows there are some children whose fathers can't come. She probably forgot to mention it. What about Katy Dickson? Her daddy's in the navy, and he probably won't get permission to leave his ship just for that. So don't worry. I'm sure Sally didn't mean to be unkind.'

'Yes, she did,' Holly said quickly.

'Sally doesn't like me, 'cause I can skate better than her,' she added as more tears overflowed to trace two separate paths down her cheeks.

Autumn reached out and pulled Holly's unresisting body into her arms. Her own throat suddenly felt raw and painful, and she blinked away the tears stinging her eyes. She kissed Holly's hair and gently rocked the child, unsure for a moment who was comforting whom.

'Maybe I could ask Uncle Matt.' The words were muffled against her cheek, but Autumn had no problem deciphering them. Her heart skipped a beat, and as she started to return Holly to the passenger seat, she tried to keep her voice even.

'I'm not sure that's a good idea,' she said as she busied herself fastening Holly's seat belt.

'But he told me he wanted to come and watch me again sometime.' Holly sniffed and gave a little hiccup. 'Please, can I ask him?'

Autumn reached into the back seat for the box of tissues she kept there, hesitating before responding to Holly's request. She knew what Matt's answer would be, but there was no guarantee that when the father-and-daughter night arrived, Matt would still be around. With careful deliberation she wiped Holly's nose and eyes. 'We don't know how long Uncle Matt is planning on staying. He may not even be here.'

'But can I ask him?' Holly repeated with barely concealed eagerness.

'All right,' Autumn relented, and was rewarded with a watery smile.

'Are we going home now?' Holly asked as Autumn started the engine and drove away from the rink.

'Ah, not right away,' Autumn said as the memory of her confrontation with Matt returned. Emotionally she still felt bruised and battered by the encounter, and she had no desire to see him. 'I thought we might pop in and see Jennifer and her dad. We have a picnic to plan, remember?'

'Oh, boy, a picnic. Can we go tomorrow?' Holly asked, the last remnants of her sadness vanishing.

'We'll see,' Autumn replied before glancing over her shoulder and pulling the car into the flow of traffic.

By the time they reached the row of town houses where Linc and Jennifer lived, Autumn was beginning to have second thoughts about her spur-of-the-moment decision to pay them a visit.

Though she considered Linc a friend, she'd rarely dropped in on him like this. Holly often stayed to play with Jennifer or vice versa, but whenever Autumn arrived to collect Holly, she'd politely refused Linc's invitation to stay for a drink or a meal.

She turned to Holly, wishing now she'd suggested they have lunch at a restaurant instead, but Holly was already out of the car.

By the time Autumn joined her daughter on the sidewalk, Holly had pressed the doorbell.

The door opened to reveal Linc,

wearing a red sport shirt and white shorts. 'Autumn . . . Holly! Well, this is a surprise.'

'Hello, Linc.' Autumn saw a look of pleasure and something more come into his eyes, and for the second time in as many minutes she found herself wishing she hadn't been so intent on avoiding Matt. 'We came to see how Jennifer is doing.'

'And to tell her about the picnic tomorrow,' Holly piped up excitedly.

'A picnic tomorrow sounds wonderful,' Linc agreed easily. 'She'll love that. She's upstairs in her room, Holly. Why don't you run up and tell her all about it.' He stepped aside to let them enter.

'Okay,' Holly said, and with a smile she scampered off toward the staircase.

Linc turned to Autumn. 'Please come in. I was in the kitchen making lunch. Would you and Holly like to join us?'

'Thanks, but we really can't stay. Mrs. Brady is expecting us,' Autumn quickly improvised as she followed Linc into the bright orange and white kitchen.

In the center of the room was a work island, and scattered across its wooden surface was a colorful variety of fruits: ripe peaches and pears cut and quartered, a honeydew melon cut into bite-size pieces and several small bunches of plump green grapes. Two bowls, waiting to be filled, sat on the counter.

'Fresh fruit salad,' Linc said unnecessarily. 'Since her bout with the flu, Jennifer doesn't have much of her appetite yet. But she loves fruit.'

'Holly does, too,' Autumn commented, feeling more than a little awkward.

Linc turned and studied her for a long moment. 'Is there something wrong, Autumn?'

'Wrong? Why do you ask?'

Linc shook his head and smiled. 'In all the time I've known you, my dear, you have never just dropped in,' he pointed out calmly. 'So why today? Why now?'

'I told you. To make arrangements

for the picnic.' Autumn couldn't meet his eyes and was instantly annoyed at herself for reacting so defensively.

'A phone call would have accomplished that. Give me a little credit, please,' he said as he came toward her. 'What is it? Or should I say who is it?'

Autumn blinked rapidly, trying to dispel the tears suddenly threatening to fill her eyes.

'It's Kingston, isn't it?' Linc hurried on, annoyance in every syllable. 'What's he done?'

Autumn could only shake her head in denial, but Linc wouldn't be put off.

'I sensed something was wrong last night when he hauled you off into the corridor.' His tone was heavy with remembered anger. 'And then later when he insisted he'd take you home. I didn't pursue it because I didn't want to create a scene. What was it all about?'

Autumn couldn't believe what she was hearing. She hardly recognized the man before her — he was acting like a jealous lover.

'Dammit, Autumn, if he's done something to hurt you . . . ' Linc's hands came up to gently clasp her shoulders. 'Please tell me what's wrong. Let me help. I care about you. I care about you a great deal.'

Autumn's head shot up at his words, and she stared at him with a mixture of shock and dismay. 'Linc . . . I had no idea . . . ' She took a step back. Immediately his hands fell away, and she heard him sigh.

'It's all right, Autumn. You don't have to say anything.' He ran a hand through his hair. 'I know my timing is all wrong, but I'd hoped that maybe one day — '

'Linc, please . . . don't.' She took another step back and then turned from him, dazed and confused by what he'd said. A kind and considerate man, she'd admired the way he'd coped with the loss of his wife, admired the time, love and effort he'd put into taking care of Jennifer. She considered him a friend, a good friend. But that was all. Not for a moment had she suspected that his feelings for her were anything more.

'I'm sorry, Autumn. I didn't mean to upset you,' Linc said softly. 'Forget what I said. Just tell me what's wrong. I'll do anything — '

'Please!' Autumn's head was beginning to pound. She felt cornered and completely bewildered by the turn of events. It had been a mistake to come here. She saw that clearly now, and all she wanted was to be gone.

The sound of running footsteps reached them, and it was with a sharp sense of relief that Autumn turned to see Jennifer and Holly in the doorway.

'We're hungry, Daddy,' Jennifer informed her father before smiling warmly at Autumn.

'I'm afraid Holly and I have to be going now, Jennifer,' Autumn said, keeping her eyes averted from Linc.

'But, Mom! We just got here,' Holly protested.

'I'm sorry, darling, but it's time to

go,' Autumn insisted, trying to keep her voice steady.

'We can play tomorrow at the picnic,' Jennifer said. 'We're still going on the picnic, aren't we?'

'Of course,' came Linc's reply. 'We'll pick up Holly and Autumn at ten o'clock, if that's all right?'

Two pairs of eyes regarded Autumn anxiously, and, as much as she wanted to, she didn't have the heart to deny the girls the outing they'd been promised. 'Ten is fine,' she said, even managing to smile.

★   ★   ★

'Will Uncle Matt be at home?' Holly asked as Autumn started the car after leaving Linc and Jennifer's house.

'I don't know,' Autumn replied, all the while sending up a silent prayer that he wouldn't be. She'd had enough for one day.

To her relief there was no sign of Matt anywhere when they arrived home. Holly disappeared into the kitchen in search of Mrs. Brady and lunch, but Autumn wasn't hungry. Slowly she made her way to her room.

Kicking off her shoes, she lay down on the peach-colored bedspread and gently began to massage the throbbing pain at her temples. Her world seemed to be falling about her ears, and she was at a loss to know what to do about it. She had never felt so alone before . . .

No, that was a lie. She moaned and closed her eyes, willing the memory suddenly oozing through the crack in her defenses back into the dark reaches of her mind, but it refused to comply.

So vivid was the scene playing through her mind, it could have happened yesterday.

Dr. Bentley had just informed her she was pregnant. She couldn't remember leaving his office, couldn't remember collapsing in the hospital corridor outside. She'd come out of the fainting spell to find herself in the nurses' lounge, staring into the anxious eyes of another trainee nurse who'd asked her if she could call her family or a friend.

But there had been no one to call. She was alone. Alone and pregnant.

How could she have let it happen? She was training to be a nurse for heaven's sake! She knew the facts of life, knew exactly what the consequences of those unforgettable moments with Matt might be. How could she have been so naive to think it wouldn't happen to her? Now, as a wave of pain, and longing swirled through her, Autumn curled her body into a tight ball.

* * *

She hadn't believed that such a thing as love at first sight existed . . . until Matt walked into her life. When he came to stay next door with Paul that summer, he hardly seemed to notice her, but she fell hopelessly, helplessly, in love with him.

Matt was the most handsome man she'd ever seen, and every chance she got she slipped next door to pay a visit. Matt was kind and polite, totally unaware that whenever he glanced her way or spoke, her heart would flutter madly against her rib cage as though trying to escape.

She thought of him continually throughout the year that followed, and when he returned the next summer she prayed that this time he would notice her.

The fact that she was in the midst of her training course as a nurse and living in residence proved to be more than a little frustrating. Working at the hospital and studying took up most of her time, but on the pretext of visiting Paul, she'd managed to see Matt.

During the past year she had made the transition from a young girl into a young woman, and with unbridled excitement she hoped that Matt, too, would notice how she'd changed.

It came as a wonderful surprise to find him waiting for her outside the hospital one evening when she came off duty. At the sight of him leaning casually against a beautiful white convertible, she had to consciously slow her pace for fear she'd appear too eager.

For the next three weeks she spent every spare moment she had with Matt. During those weeks her life was one mad, hectic rush. Her mother moved to Florida to live with her sister and, wanting to complete her training in Vancouver, Autumn found herself in the throes of trying to find an apartment near the hospital, as well as a fellow nurse with whom to share expenses.

There weren't enough hours in the day for all she had to do, but she couldn't bring herself to waste precious time scanning bulletin boards or advertisements, not when she could be with Matt.

He was always the perfect gentleman: attentive, charming and a good listener. With only a smile he could tie her heart in knots, and whenever he touched her — a fingertip across her cheek, a teasing kiss — she felt a hunger build inside her that was strange, frightening and wonderful all at the same time.

His kisses were all too brief and usually left her eager for more. She'd never felt like this about anyone before. She was in love. She was sure of it.

The picnic to celebrate the fact that she passed the tough midterms was Matt's idea. Not only did he insist on providing the basket of food and a bottle of champagne, he arranged for the use of a friend's cabin and a secluded stretch of beach.

For two days prior to the picnic she could hardly think of anything else. When Matt told her he'd invited Paul and a friend along, Autumn was hard-pressed to hide her disappointment, and couldn't help wishing Paul had declined Matt's invitation.

On the afternoon of the picnic her wish came true. Paul came down with a virus. Autumn expressed her concern, but inwardly her heart danced at the prospect of spending the afternoon and evening alone with Matt.

In his black bathing suit Matt was the epitome of every woman's romantic fantasy. They spent several hours swimming and sunbathing, and she could hardly keep her eyes off him.

As they lay on the blanket enjoying the delicious barbecued salmon, caesar salad and garlic bread from the picnic hamper, Autumn wondered exactly what Matt's feelings were toward her. He enjoyed being with her, that much she knew, but whenever he held her or kissed her, she sensed a tension in him, as if he was holding back.

She stole a glance at him then, and her breath caught in her throat at the look smoldering in the depths of those wondrous blue eyes. Her whole body seemed to grow hot under his gaze. She ached to reach out, touch, taste and explore the firm contours of his body, to feel the strength of his arms around her, to know the mastery of his kiss.

Matt, on the other hand, seemed unaffected. When they finished their meal, he hopped quickly to his feet and mumbled that it was time to pack up and leave.

A feeling of disappointment washed over Autumn. She rose to her feet, deflated by the fact that Matt appeared to be in a hurry to end the outing.

She wasn't sure just what prompted her actions — a mixture of annoyance and disappointment perhaps — but as Matt bent over to gather the beach blanket, she came up behind him and gave him a push. Caught completely off guard, he toppled over onto the blanket.

At the shocked expression on his face, Autumn couldn't contain the laughter bubbling to the surface. Suddenly without warning, she found herself on her back looking up at Matt, unsure exactly how she'd gotten there.

Her laughter died instantly and her breath froze in her lungs at the blatant desire she could see in Matt's blue eyes. Tiny explosions of excitement erupted deep inside her, and as his lips came down on hers, she almost moaned aloud at the wonder of it.

At first his mouth was warm and pliant and delightfully sensual, but as he deepened the kiss, he drew from her a response that shattered her soul.

She couldn't think; she could only feel, as a kaleidoscope of sensations coursed through her, leaving in their wake an urgent need for more. She was a willing participant, held captive in a ring of fire they'd ignited together.

I love you! Her heart cried out its silent message, and trustingly she followed Matt through a magical maze, where at every corner she made a breathless discovery that sent her spinning faster and faster into the white-hot center of the universe.

She had never known such joy, such fulfillment, and when she lay exhausted in his arms, she began to dream about the future.

Later, as Matt drove back to town, she was so full of wonder at what they had shared she hardly spoke. Matt, too, was silent, his expression thoughtful, and not until they reached the nurses' residence did she learn the reason for his silence.

Calmly, and without any outward emotion, he apologized for losing control. Then he went on to tell her that he was leaving for Europe in a matter of hours. Too shocked and hurt to speak, she stared at him in utter amazement, unable to believe what she was hearing.

All she could think about was the fact that what they had just shared had obviously meant nothing to Matt — he was leaving!

Though his voice droned on, she was too numb with pain to fully comprehend everything he was saying. A few scattered fragments — she was young, her career was only beginning, he was trying to be fair — were some of the words she remembered. But embedded in her heart was the fleeting kiss and the softly spoken promise that he'd call.

She didn't know how she made it through the days that followed. When she began to experience bouts of sickness and a general feeling of lethargy, she made an appointment with one of the hospital doctors.

When the doctor gave her the news, all she could think about, at first, was what her pregnancy would mean to her life and her career. She felt no joy, no wonder, no excitement — those feelings all came later as the thought of having Matt's child began to sink in.

She firmly believed that as the child's father, Matt should be told — he had a right to know. But the pain of his departure was still too close to the surface, and so she put off the task.

When she ran into Paul in the hospital corridor a few days later, the simple pleasure of seeing a friend made her forget her troubles, but only for a moment.

Paul was quick to guess her predicament, and though he agreed to her request to track Matt down and leave a message asking him to call her, his attitude was less than encouraging. And when she in turn discovered that Paul's own situation was infinitely worse than hers, her troubles suddenly seemed insignificant.

As she waited to hear from Matt, there formed between herself and Paul what she could only describe as a mutual support system. It was only a few short weeks later, with no word from Matt, that Paul proposed, laying out the terms of what he called a marriage of convenience. She accepted, knowing that if she wanted to keep her baby, she had no other choice, and knowing that Paul had even fewer choices left to him.

★　★　★

Autumn angrily wiped away the tears brought on by the memories and eased herself off the bed. Snatching a tissue from the box on the dressing table, she blew her nose and gently dabbed the moisture from her eyes.

Matt's presence had ripped open old

wounds and reawakened memories and dreams best forgotten. But he couldn't stay forever. She would just have to be patient, try to avoid further confrontations and hope that he would leave them in peace.

As she made her way downstairs, she knew her wish was totally unrealistic, but she found she was unwilling at the moment to even think about what Matt's next move might be, now that he knew Holly was his daughter.

6

Autumn spent the remainder of the afternoon playing with Holly. She usually enjoyed their time together, but today her thoughts kept drifting to Matt. Where had he gone? What was he doing?

Holly, too, seemed out of sorts, not her usual energetic self, and Autumn sensed she was anxious for Matt to return. By the time they sat down to a light supper, there was still no sign of him, but instead of feeling relieved, Autumn found the tension inside her building.

As she was putting Holly to bed, the child voiced the question circling incessantly in her own head.

'Where's Uncle Matt? Why didn't he come back for supper?'

'I don't know, sweetheart,' Autumn replied as she closed the book of fairy tales she'd been reading to Holly.

'I wanted to ask him about the skating night,' Holly went on. 'Do you think he'll come?' she asked. Blue eyes, so like Matt's, regarded her earnestly.

'I can't answer that, darling. I'm sorry, but you'll have to ask Uncle Matt.' At her words Holly's face fell, and Autumn felt her heart contract.

'He hasn't gone, has he? He wouldn't leave without saying goodbye, would he?' There were tears in Holly's eyes now. A loving and generous child, she'd obviously given her trust to Matt, and Autumn could only pray it wasn't misplaced.

'Of course not,' she quickly assured her. 'He's probably visiting friends,' she improvised, trying not to think about another time when he'd left equally as abruptly.

'Good night, Mummy,' Holly said as she snuggled beneath the comforter.

Autumn kissed her daughter. 'Good night, darling,' she said softly. Rising from the bed, she crossed to the door, but as she reached for the light switch, Holly spoke again.

'Could you ask Uncle Matt to come in and kiss me good-night when he gets back?'

Autumn's hand trembled slightly as she flicked the switch. She turned toward the bed, glad of the shadows that helped to hide the tears suddenly stinging her eyes. 'I'll ask him,' she managed to say before closing the door behind her.

Downstairs in the living room, she crossed to the bar and poured herself a glass of Perrier. The day had been both traumatic and eventful, and as she sipped the cool, refreshing liquid, she felt the tension inside her slowly begin to ease.

That Matt had won Holly's affection and trust so quickly surprised Autumn. While Paul had never been blatantly cruel or unkind to Holly, their relationship hadn't been particularly close.

Autumn realized that from an early age Holly had instinctively sensed that

Paul had little patience and even less understanding of the needs of a child.

He was affectionate toward her only when the purpose suited him. There were times that he found her antics a welcome distraction, sometimes highly amusing, but for the most part Autumn had had her work cut out keeping Holly out of Paul's way.

An easygoing, happy child, Holly had taken Paul's haphazard treatment in her stride, a fact Autumn had often marveled at. It was a rare occasion when Paul had allowed the child into his studio to watch him paint, and she would always behave beautifully, as if she somehow knew the treat would be short-lived should she misbehave.

In contrast, Matt, after only a few short hours, had managed to firmly establish himself in Holly's affections, a fact that greatly troubled Autumn. For when Matt left, as he would eventually, Holly would be the one who would be hurt.

Annoyed, Autumn turned and walked

to the window, staring out at the mountains silhouetted against the evening sky.

A feeling of tiredness swept over her, and she downed the remainder of the Perrier before returning the glass to the bar.

Where was he? Was it possible the truth had driven him away? No. That was simply wishful thinking. He'd be back.

So why was she waiting and worrying? a tiny voice asked. He was a grown man, capable of looking after himself. Decisively now she turned off the table lamp and moved to the door, and at that same moment she heard the sound of tires on the gravel driveway.

She hadn't realized she was holding her breath until the outer door opened and Matt appeared. Her lungs emptied in a rush of air, and her heart leaped at the sight of him.

Matt closed the door and leaned heavily against it. His gaze was immediately drawn to the figure standing in the muted shadows of the doorway to the living room. He saw the tension in her body, the look of fatigue on her face, and the embers of an emotion he'd carefully buried in that secret place in his heart flared to life.

After she'd stormed out earlier, his first impulse had been to go out and get drunk, but by the time the cab he'd called dropped him downtown, his anger and outrage had been replaced by a growing wonder and inordinate joy that Holly was indeed his daughter, his own flesh and blood.

The emotions that had stampeded through him had been like nothing he'd ever known before. He'd wanted to laugh and cry at the same time, to shout to the world that he had a child.

But as he'd sat in the bar nursing the drink he'd ordered, his euphoria had quickly worn off. Autumn had deceived him, kept the truth about Holly from him, and for that he wanted to hate her. But how could he hate the woman who was the mother of his child? Hate was a destructive emotion, and he wanted nothing to jeopardize the relationship blossoming between him and Holly.

'I'm afraid you missed dinner,' Autumn said now, cutting through his thoughts. He watched as she crossed the carpeted hall toward the staircase.

'I lost track of time,' he told her. 'I guess I should have called. I'm sorry.' Matt could see she was in a hurry to leave, and suddenly he wanted her to stay. 'Would there by any chance be any leftovers? I'm starving.'

Autumn stopped and looked at Matt. As her glance collided with his, she felt her pulse accelerate and a familiar weakness invade her limbs. 'I can rustle you up something, if you like,' she said, and moved on toward the kitchen.

Though he was more than capable of finding something to appease his hunger, Matt was content to let Autumn play hostess. As he followed her into the kitchen, the subtle yet tantalizing fragrance of her perfume floated enticingly around him. It was the delicate scent of roses and wisteria, a scent that was hers alone, and as much a part of his memory of her as everything else about her.

Autumn opened the refrigerator door. 'There's some cold meat and salad,' she told him as she reached inside.

'Sounds great,' Matt answered, moving to the round table by the window that looked out onto a patio. Slipping off his jacket, he dropped it over the back of one of the chairs, and with his eyes on Autumn, he sat down.

She was beautiful. The shirt dress she wore was the color of a ripe orange and hugged every subtle curve and elegant contour of her slender body. He watched in fascination as she arranged slices of meat and wedges of cheese and tomato on a plate. Her hair hung loose about her shoulders, its yellow and gold highlights reminding him of fallen autumn leaves.

He closed his eyes, and instantly there flashed into his mind that image of Autumn lying naked on the sand, her arms reaching out for him. He felt his body tense as a need sharp and strong made its presence known. Perspiration broke out on his forehead as he realized that even after all this time he could still recall the silken touch of her hair against his skin. He had to force himself to relax, to bank the fire racing through him. Why had he never been able to forget her? he asked for the millionth time.

'If you want more, please help yourself,' Autumn said as she crossed to the table.

She'd been all too conscious of his scrutiny, and it was not without some effort that she had managed to keep her hands from trembling. Her goal now was to leave, but as she set the plate, knife and fork on the table his hand closed over her wrist.

'Don't go.' Matt's soft tone caused her heart to kick against her ribs in alarm, and beneath his fingers heat began to spread.

'I — I'm tired. It's been a long

day — ' She stumbled over the words, fighting panic and something else she was afraid to define. She tried to pull away, but the action only served to bring Matt to his feet.

Dear God! She couldn't breathe. He was much too close. Had her heart stopped beating? She found she wasn't sure of anything but the need to put some distance between them.

Her body, however, refused to obey her urgent commands to move away, and as his breath stirred the tendrils of her hair, it was all she could do not to lay her head against his chest and seek the comfort she hadn't even known she craved.

She closed her eyes against the longing that assailed her, and with the last of her strength she broke free. Her breathing was ragged as she headed for the door.

'Tell me about Holly. Please . . . '

The words stopped her cold, and she had to bite down on the inner softness of her mouth to stifle the cry that sprung to her lips. Slowly, painfully, she turned around.

If he'd ordered her, or even shouted his demands, she could have ignored him and walked out. But there was no mistaking the fact that the plea came directly from his heart.

'What, ah, what is it you want to know?' she asked.

'Everything.' His eyes held her captive and, as if drawn by some invisible force, she began to make her way back toward the table.

She sat down, and resting her hands on the table, she clasped them together to stop them from shaking. He sank into the chair next to her, and she thought she heard him sigh.

She wasn't sure how to begin, but a quick glance at Matt earned her a slight smile of encouragement, and she caught a glimmer of something she couldn't decipher in the depths of his eyes.

Matt hadn't been sure she'd stay, and the relief he felt when she returned to the table was immense. As he waited for her to speak, he sensed a definite change in the atmosphere. The tension was still there, but overriding it was a feeling of harmony, tentative perhaps, but it was there, and Holly was the reason for it. As her mother and father, they shared a special bond, a bond that nothing could change, and with that thought, a feeling of happiness settled around his heart.

Although hesitant at first, Autumn slowly began to tell Matt about his daughter's early years. She told him when Holly started to crawl, when she took her first step, what her favorite toy had been, and that she'd loved to play peekaboo.

Memories and moments kept spilling out. She recounted the time Holly, wearing only a pair of rubber boots and a diaper, had wandered outside to play in the rain. And she told him about how sick Holly had been when she'd contracted chicken pox.

Matt hung on her every word,

watching Autumn's changing expressions as she related numerous stories, some sad, some humorous. She was relaxed now, totally at ease, and as he listened he found himself wishing the friendship blossoming between them would strengthen and grow.

He hadn't realized until this moment how much he had missed being with her. When he'd dated her that summer, so long ago she'd looked so young and eager, yet he'd caught a look of vulnerability in her pale blue eyes. She'd been unaware of her own femininity, her own sensuality, and for the first time in his life he'd felt protective toward a woman. But more than that he'd been completely captivated by her simple joy of life, her energy, her drive and her total lack of guile. He'd never laughed so much, lived so much, felt so much as when he was with her.

Now, with a sudden insight that surprised him, Matt realized how empty his life had been during the past five years. He had his career, and he'd convinced himself that was enough. But important as his career was, there had been times he'd had to fight a certain restlessness, a feeling that something was missing.

'Good heavens, look at the time,' Autumn's exclamation brought Matt out of his reverie. He watched her as she gathered up his plate and the two coffee cups.

'You've done a wonderful job raising Holly,' Matt said, and Autumn felt her face flush with pleasure at his words. Paul had made it clear from the moment Holly was born that the child was her responsibility.

As she'd talked, Matt had listened attentively, interrupting only to ask a brief question or make a comment. She'd been surprised at how easy it was just talking to him and she discovered that recounting a few of the more fearful moments in Holly's young life somehow acted as a form of catharsis. And from that came the realization she

133

was in grave danger of falling under Matt's spell once more.

He'd shown her a side of himself she hadn't seen before, but it was a side she wasn't altogether sure she could trust. Holly's happiness was her primary concern, and while she understood Matt's interest, it was entirely probable he would conveniently forget about his daughter as easily as he had forgotten about her. The thought sobered her.

Matt saw the play of emotions flit across Autumn's features. He could almost feel her withdrawal and he wondered at its cause.

For the past two hours, she'd shared some of the important and memorable moments of Holly's life, but now the closeness was gone, and he felt as if he'd been set adrift on a sea of loneliness with no means of reaching shore.

'It's late. I'm tired. Good night.' She sounded as cool and distant as a stranger, and Matt felt a heaviness close around his heart as he watched her walk to the door.

She hesitated for a moment, then turned. 'Oh . . . Holly wanted you to stop in and kiss her good-night.'

Matt's throat clogged with emotion. 'I — I think I can handle that,' he said, wondering if he'd ever get over the feeling of love that swamped him each time he thought of Holly. 'Autumn . . . ' She was leaving, but there was something he needed to say.

'Yes?' She braced herself against the door, trying to ignore the way her pulse had kicked into high gear when he'd spoken her name.

'Thank you.' Their eyes met and held for what seemed an interminable second, and in that moment Autumn felt the icy wall around her heart melt away.

She quickly left and went upstairs. In her room she undressed and climbed into bed. The day had been full of unwelcome surprises, but somehow she'd weathered them. As she lay back against the pillows, she wondered once more about the feeling of closeness she'd experienced as she'd sat with Matt in the kitchen.

And when she heard the familiar creak of Holly's bedroom door opening, she couldn't stop the smile that curled at the corners of her mouth.

7

'We're going on a picnic. We're going on a picnic.'

It was Holly's excited chant outside his bedroom that woke Matt the next morning. Slipping on his robe, he crossed to the door and opened it. Holly, wearing blue shorts and a matching T-shirt, her blond hair tied in a ponytail, grinned engagingly up at him.

'Good morning! What's all this noise about?' he asked with mock severity as he tightened the sash of his robe.

Holly kept on grinning. 'Aren't you coming, too?' she asked.

'Where?'

'On the picnic,' Holly replied. 'Uncle Linc and Jennifer will be here soon,' she told him. 'You'll have to get dressed.'

'You mean I can't go like this?' Matt asked.

The sound of Holly's laughter filled the hallway, making him smile, and he fought the urge to haul her into his arms and hold her tightly against him.

'What's going on?' Autumn asked as she emerged from her room across the hall. Her eyes darted to Matt, and at the sight of him wearing only a terry cloth bathrobe, her heart went into a tailspin. She could see the fine dark hairs on his chest curling at the neckline of his robe, and her breath caught in her throat. The smile on his face was for Holly, she told herself, but that didn't diffuse its devastating effect one iota. If her feelings for him had died, then why did she react so strongly whenever he was near?

Matt, in turn, felt his pulse take a giant leap. Autumn looked great, he thought as he let his glance slide over her. She wore a bright green blouse tucked into the waistline of a multicolored skirt that fell gracefully over her hips and swirled about her legs to end just below her knees. Her hair was drawn away from her face, twisted into one long braid that hung over her right shoulder and reached almost to the tip of her breast.

'You'll have to hurry, Uncle Matt. You slept in.' Holly's voice effectively cut into his thoughts, and he shifted his gaze back to the child.

'What time is it?' he asked.

'Picnic time,' came the cheeky reply.

'Of course,' he said, laughing. 'Would you mind if I joined you?'

Autumn quickly schooled her features, meeting his gaze with a coolness she was far from feeling. Inside she was fighting to keep the memory of the picnic she'd shared with Matt from surfacing. 'By all means, join us,' she said, her tone polite.

'We love picnics, don't we, Mummy?' Holly was saying.

'Yes,' Autumn managed, dropping her gaze to the child.

'I'll be with you in two shakes of a . . . pony's tail,' Matt said as he reached out and tugged gently on

Holly's ponytail.

Holly giggled. 'You're silly, Uncle Matt.'

Matt grinned back at her. 'You're right,' he said, then glanced back to Autumn. 'Don't leave without me!'

Under the warm spray of the shower, Matt found his thoughts lingering on Autumn, back to those moments in the kitchen the previous evening. As he'd listened to her talk about Holly, he'd felt a closeness, a warm contentment and a feeling of belonging. For the first time he'd realized that these were the things missing from his life, and an ache of longing had stabbed at his heart.

He'd lain awake for most of the night, and in the darkness his thoughts had drifted back to the fateful day he'd made love to Autumn. He'd been astonished at how quickly he'd lost control, but the emotions she'd aroused in him had been like nothing he'd ever known before.

He'd kept reminding himself that at

twenty she was young, inexperienced and very vulnerable. She was just starting out in her career, at the brink of discovering her own potential, and it was for this reason he'd made the decision to walk away, leaving her free to pursue the challenges and goals she had set for herself.

But through his own stupidity and misguided intentions, he'd allowed her to slip through his fingers, and a feeling of regret overwhelmed him.

But there were still too many unanswered questions. Why hadn't she tried to contact him and tell him she was pregnant? Had she been playing him for the fool, as he'd accused her, and been seeing Paul, as well? Had she lied to Paul and told him he was the child's father? Was that why he'd married her? He shook his head, unable to believe in his heart that she was the kind of woman who used men.

Besides, she hadn't needed to lie. Paul had been obsessed with Autumn, that much Matt had seen with his own eyes. And perhaps he was simply looking for an answer he could live with instead of facing the truth that she'd been in love with Paul when she married him. After all, hadn't they been friends long before he'd appeared on the scene?

Matt pondered on this as he turned off the water and reached for the towel on the rail. But as he stepped from the shower, he couldn't shake the feeling that the pieces of the puzzle didn't quite fit.

He pulled on jeans and a sweatshirt, wincing a little as he walked to the dressing table. As he ran a comb through his hair, he turned his thoughts to Holly.

That she was his daughter was a bonus he'd never dreamed of, and as a feeling of warmth and love spread through him, he vowed that he was going to play an important role in her life.

'Can we go now? Can we?' two excited, young voices greeted Matt as he descended the stairs.

Matt nodded briefly to Linc as he emerged with Autumn from the kitchen. Between them they were carrying a large old-fashioned wicker picnic basket.

'Looks like we're all ready,' Matt said, addressing the two girls. 'Introduce me to your friend, Holly,' he added, as he reached the bottom step.

'This is Jennifer,' Holly said.

'Hello, Jennifer. I'm Holly's Uncle Matt.'

'Let's get this show on the road,' Linc said, though by his tone Autumn sensed he wasn't pleased that Matt was accompanying them.

Jennifer's presence had helped to ease the awkwardness Autumn felt when Linc arrived, and she was thankful that he made no reference to their conversation of the previous day.

Holly and Jennifer insisted on sitting in the front seat with Linc, leaving Autumn with no alternative but to sit in the back with Matt. She kept her attention focused on the passing scenery, pretending an interest she didn't feel.

It was a beautiful day for late September, and ideal for a picnic. The sun shone brightly, slipping occasionally behind the fluffy white clouds dancing by.

Linc drove across the Lions Gate Bridge and onto the Stanley Park Causeway. The girls talked and giggled, unaware of the tension slowly building inside Autumn.

Beside her, Matt seemed totally relaxed, and she found this unnerving. His nearness was acutely disturbing, and each time he glanced her way her heart accelerated in response.

As the car joined the procession making its way around the famous park, Autumn noticed that quite a number of Vancouver's residents had decided to take advantage of what would probably be one of the few remaining sunny days of the summer. Minutes later Linc pulled into a parking space behind the zoo.

'Hooray! Hooray!' chorused the children as they quickly undid their seat belts and jumped out into the sunshine.

'Can we go and look for a picnic table?' Holly asked excitedly.

'Are we going to see the animals first?' Jennifer wanted to know.

'Can we have an ice cream?' they chimed together.

Matt joined the children on the sidewalk. 'Why don't we look for a good picnic spot while your mother and Linc unload the car?' he proposed.

His suggestion was greeted with shouts of agreement from the girls. Matt obviously intended to have a good time and seemed totally at ease with the children. As Autumn's eyes met Matt's she found it difficult not to respond to the laughter lurking there.

'That's a good idea,' Linc said as he moved to the rear of the car. 'Autumn and I can manage. We'll catch up.'

'Great!' Matt replied, and holding out a hand to each child, they set off.

'I hope you don't mind, Autumn,' Linc said as he unlocked the trunk. 'I'm rather glad of the chance to talk to you alone.' He reached in and withdrew the picnic basket.

Autumn's heart sank. She'd hoped after her shocked reaction the day before that Linc wouldn't pursue the matter, at least not now. She sighed. 'Linc, I think of you as a friend . . . '

Linc reached out to touch her arm. 'It's all right, Autumn. Don't look so worried.' He gave her a rueful smile. 'If friendship is all you feel, I'll settle for that,' he added as he leaned toward her and kissed her cheek.

'Hey, Mom!' Holly's shout made Autumn jump. She turned to see Matt and the girls bearing down on them. 'We found a terrific spot just over there.' Holly pointed back the way they had come. 'There's a picnic table and everything,' she went on.

'But we have to hurry before someone else picks it,' Jennifer added.

'We're coming,' Linc said, reaching into the trunk of the car once more.

Matt joined them at the car, mumbling under his breath. He'd seen

Linc lean over and kiss Autumn, and the emotion that clawed at his insides was easily definable. To Matt the gesture appeared both loving and intimate, and he'd had to fight the desire to rush over and tear Linc Armstrong away from Autumn.

Autumn threw Matt a questioning glance. He was angry. She could tell by his taut features and the dark look on his face. Surely his reaction wasn't the result of having witnessed the kiss Linc had bestowed on her? At that thought her heart suddenly skipped a beat. Annoyed now, she silently scolded herself for even entertaining such a foolish notion.

'You can carry this,' Linc said, handing Jennifer a beach ball and a Frisbee. 'Here, Autumn!' He held out a large tartan blanket.

'What about me, Uncle Linc?' Holly asked eagerly.

'You can help your Uncle Matt with the picnic basket. I'll lock the car and bring a couple of folding chairs. We can come for the other chairs if we need them.'

Autumn followed Matt and Holly to the spot the children had chosen. She smiled as she watched her daughter help Matt put the basket on the picnic table.

Taking the blanket, she began to spread it out on the grass. She was surprised when Matt appeared at her side to help, and when his hand accidentally brushed hers, a sensation much like a tiny electric shock danced along her arm, leaving in its wake a tingling warmth.

Startled, Autumn let go of the blanket, and then instinctively made a grab for it. That action caused her to stumble against him, almost knocking them both over. His hand shot out to steady her, and instantly she was aware of a dizzying heat spiraling through her.

Lifting her gaze to his, she saw that his mouth was a mere kiss away. Her heartbeat roared in her ears like a thundering waterfall, and the heat steadily consuming her seemed to reach a fever pitch wherever their bodies touched.

A need she'd forgotten how to feel, a desire she'd never thought she'd know again, rose like a tidal wave to overwhelm her, and it was all she could do not to close the gap between them.

'Careful!' Matt's softly spoken admonishment fanned her face and sent fresh echoes of need racing through her.

'I'm all right.' Her tone wasn't in the least convincing, but before Matt could move, she jerked out of his arms and hurried toward the picnic table where Linc and the children were busy smoothing out a tablecloth.

Matt could only stare after Autumn, trying unsuccessfully to deal with emotions suddenly gone awry. He hadn't been sure what he'd seen in the depths of her eyes just then, but during those endless seconds the desire to kiss her had been almost irresistible. As he watched her scurry away, he knew that if they'd been alone, he would have readily given in to the need still running rampant within him.

Thoughtfully Matt finished spreading the blanket on the grass, then turned to the girls. 'Want to play a game?' he asked.

The twosome immediately came running.

'What game?' Holly asked.

'Do you know how to play Donkey?' he asked, and bent to retrieve the large beach ball.

'No. How do you play?' Jennifer asked, making a grab for the ball, but Matt held it out of reach.

'It's a game of catch. Come on, I'll teach you,' he said as he led them a few yards away to an open space.

Autumn was relieved to see Matt walk away. The effects of her encounter with him moments ago still lingered, and she wasn't ready to face him.

From where she sat on the blanket, she watched as he carefully explained the simple game. They proceeded to play, and Autumn was amazed to see him become totally immersed in the game. She admired the way he engineered the loss of the first game, thus having to be the one to pay the forfeit, which simply amounted to hee-hawing like a donkey.

The girls doubled over with laughter, and Autumn found it difficult to keep a straight face herself. He seemed so relaxed and at ease with the children, and they were both enchanted with him and his antics.

She knew some men had difficulty relating to children. Paul would never have participated in children's games, but Matt appeared to have no such reservations, and for a moment she felt a pang of regret at what he had missed.

She quickly thrust those thoughts aside as Linc, who'd returned to the car for Jennifer's sweater, lowered himself onto the blanket beside her.

'Penny for your thoughts,' he said with a smile.

'I was just thinking about how nice it

is to have the weekend off,' she improvised.

'But you enjoy your work, don't you?' Linc said.

'I love it,' she replied enthusiastically.

'Love what?' Matt's voice cut in.

Autumn's head jerked up, and she was surprised to find Mart frowning down at her. She averted her gaze, fighting to control a heart that was suddenly racing.

Matt reached for one of the lounge chairs nearby. His knee was throbbing painfully.

'Come and play Donkey with us, Daddy,' Jennifer said, running to her father and tugging at his sleeve. 'Uncle Matt says he needs a rest,' she went on.

'You'll have to teach me,' Linc said as he rose from the blanket.

'It's easy,' Jennifer assured him as they moved away to join Holly.

Autumn started to get up, reluctant to be alone with Matt. 'Maybe I'll join — ' she began.

But Matt forestalled her. 'Stay and

talk to me,' he said, then grimaced as he attempted to stretch his leg.

'Are you all right?' Autumn asked, seeing the look of pain on his face.

'No, but that's par for the course these days.' He shrugged. 'Tell me what you and Linc were talking about?'

'My job at the clinic,' she said as she dropped back onto the blanket.

'What clinic?'

'David Scott's. Why?'

'Nothing, only I have an appointment with David tomorrow morning,' Matt revealed.

Autumn couldn't hide her surprise. 'Is that why you're still here?' The words were out before she thought to stop them, and she felt her face flush under his gaze.

'That's part of the reason,' he acknowledged.

'If your knee is causing you that much pain, shouldn't you be resting it?'

'I've never been one to sit around,' he said easily.

Or stay in one place too long,

Autumn thought. 'There's been no mention in the press that you're here to attend the clinic.'

'No, and that's the way I'd like to keep it,' he said. 'But by tomorrow, who knows?' He shifted in the chair, trying to find a more comfortable position. 'You're a nurse at the clinic?'

'Yes, I've been working part-time for four months,' she told him, all the while thinking that his injury must indeed be serious for him to be seeing David Scott.

'You must have finished your training, then,' Matt said. 'If my calculations are correct, you must have been about halfway through when — ' He stopped abruptly, and his eyes flew to hers.

Autumn met his gaze directly, the air between them suddenly crackling with tension. Her blue eyes never wavered, and Matt was the first to look away.

'I was halfway through my training when I found out I was pregnant,' she supplied, her voice controlled and devoid of emotion. And where were you? her heart cried silently.

Matt brought his eyes back to hers, and she could have sworn she saw a look of pain and regret in their blue depths.

'Mummy! Mummy! We're hungry.' Holly's arrival effectively cut through the heavy silence that had descended between them.

Dragging her eyes away from Matt, Autumn jumped to her feet. 'Then let's eat!' she said, wishing just for a moment that Holly hadn't interrupted. She felt sure Matt had been about to say something, to perhaps explain why he'd ignored her request that he call. Fool! she chastised herself. What good would it do now?

Autumn deliberately turned her attention to the picnic basket. She set out the feast Mrs. Brady had prepared — cold chicken, coleslaw, potato salad and potato chips, sweet pickles, buns, cheese, cherry tomatoes, lettuce and various kinds of fruits and fruit drinks — but all the while her thoughts were on Matt.

Several squirrels came to visit while they ate, and the children had fun tossing crumbs and watching the small creatures scurry across the grass to retrieve the morsels.

'Can we have an ice cream, now?' Jennifer asked her father as she hopped down from the picnic table Holly quickly joined her friend, and Autumn smiled and shook her head at the twosome.

'All right, you two. Let's go.' Linc got to his feet and tossed his paper napkin into a nearby garbage can. 'Autumn and Uncle Matt can clear away the picnic.' Linc flashed a smile at Autumn before sauntering off toward the concession stand, the girls running ahead.

Autumn glanced at Matt lying on his back on the blanket. His eyes were closed and he seemed to be dozing. Her fingers suddenly stilled in their task of gathering the paper plates, and she felt her heart skip a beat, reacting as it always did whenever she looked at him.

He was outrageously handsome, of that there was no doubt, and at age thirty there was now a maturity in his looks that only added to his attraction.

A breeze ruffled his hair, causing several strands to fall over his forehead, and instinctively her hand reached out into the empty air. She withdrew it, annoyed at her reaction, and for several minutes she concentrated on clearing away the remnants of their picnic.

But it wasn't long before her glance returned to the figure stretched out on the blanket. What was it about Matt that stirred her soul and captured her senses?

His body was that of an athlete, muscular yet exquisitely defined. And as she stared longingly at him, she suddenly found herself recalling the time when she'd experienced firsthand the fine textures of his skin, felt the muscles ripple beneath her questing fingers and known the fulfillment of a dream.

Dear God! She closed her eyes and

turned away. Being alone with Matt was becoming increasingly hazardous to her state of mind, and it was with relief that she saw Linc and the children returning.

The noise as they approached awakened Matt, and he slowly eased himself to a sitting position.

'Want some, Uncle Matt?' Holly asked, thrusting the cone at him.

'Yes, please,' he replied. The ice cream was leaning precariously to one side, dripping down the cone, and Autumn found her eyes drawn to watch as Matt, with a few flicks of his tongue, quickly restored the cone to order.

A need, painful in its intensity, coursed through her, and it took every ounce of effort to turn away.

'Autumn . . . Autumn?' Linc's hand covered hers for a moment.

'I'm sorry,' she said, turning to him.

'Are you all right? You look a little pale.' Linc studied her for a moment.

'I'm fine,' she said, and managed to smile. 'What were you saying?'

'I thought I'd take a few things back to the car. The girls want to wander around the zoo for a while. After they finish their ice cream, of course.'

'Fine,' Autumn answered. 'The picnic basket's ready.' She turned to speak to Holly, but to her surprise saw her heading toward a playground area with Matt and Jennifer. As she watched them cross the grassy area, she noticed that Matt was favoring his left leg, and a wave of sympathy washed over her, sympathy and something more, something she wasn't willing to acknowledge.

She sat down at the picnic table and tried, unsuccessfully, to sort out her feelings. Matt was a very attractive man, a fact she'd always been aware of, but while she may have thought herself in love with him that summer five-years ago, he'd turned his back on her.

She'd made the mistake of trusting blindly, of giving all she was capable of giving, and as a result she'd been burned. She had no intention of putting her hands into the same fire, or of even getting close to the flame, but she wished her resolve didn't crumble at the merest look, the briefest look. He'd broken her heart once. She'd be a fool to let it happen again.

8

Autumn's attention was suddenly distracted by the sound of a child crying. She jumped to her feet and spun around in time to see Matt hurrying toward her with Holly in his arms.

Dear God! Please let her be all right, she prayed silently as she raced to meet them. 'What happened?' she asked anxiously, willing herself not to panic as she reached for Holly.

'Don't!' Holly's plea stopped her. 'Mummy, my arm! It hurts! It hurts!' Holly's plaintive cry tore at Autumn's heart, and she had to force back the tears stinging her eyes.

'She was on the swing.' Matt's voice was full of anguish. 'She fell and landed on her arm.'

Anger shot through Autumn like a bolt of lightning. How could he have let it happen? But such thinking was unreasonable. For Holly's sake she forced herself to remain calm. 'It's all right, darling. Mummy's here,' she said in a tone that belied her inner feelings. 'Let me take a look,' she added.

'No!' Holly shouted, fear in her voice. 'Don't touch it,' she wailed, burying her face in Matt's shoulder.

'I won't, darling,' Autumn assured her as she threw an accusing glance at Matt. But when she saw the look of distress in his eyes, her anger swiftly melted and her heart filled with compassion.

'I think we'd better take her to emergency,' Matt said as Linc joined them.

'Jennifer, get the ball and the blanket. There's a good girl,' Linc said, quickly taking command. 'Matt, you'd better take Holly to the car. Here are the keys, Autumn. We'll be right behind you.'

'Let's go,' Matt said.

Autumn hurried ahead to unlock the car. She opened the rear door for Matt and moved out of his way as he gently eased Holly into the back seat.

'Be brave, sweetheart,' he said softly. 'I know it hurts, but we'll have you fixed up in no time.' He withdrew and let Autumn take the seat next to Holly.

Linc and Jennifer arrived at a run. Autumn surrendered the keys and managed to give Jennifer a smile of reassurance as the child scrambled into the front seat next to her father.

Matt had already made his way around the car and was seated on the other side of Holly. In a matter of seconds they were on their way.

The hospital was only a ten-minute drive, and throughout the journey Autumn sat with her arm around Holly, careful not to touch her injured arm. She murmured words of comfort and tried to ascertain the extent of the injury, but she was unable to determine whether or not the child's arm was broken.

'Here we are,' Linc finally said, pulling up in front of the hospital's emergency entrance.

Matt carefully eased Holly from the car, lifting her into his arms. But as she began to cry once more, a fresh wave of guilt that he hadn't been able to prevent the accident washed over him. From the moment he'd seen her fall, he'd felt as if someone had torn his heart from his body. And though he knew it was impossible, he wished he could somehow magically take away her pain.

As he followed Autumn toward the automatic doors, he found himself thinking about her reaction. He'd seen the flash of anger in her eyes and had expected an outburst . . . would even have welcomed it. But as quickly as it had come, her anger had vanished, replaced by a look of understanding and compassion, and strangely that had only compounded his guilt.

Once they were through the emergency doors, a nurse immediately came forward and led Matt to a vacant bed. 'She fell off a swing,' he explained.

'It hurts,' Holly said as Matt lowered

her onto the bed.

Autumn eased herself onto the bed beside Holly, gently holding the child against her. 'It's all right, darling. We know it hurts. But the doctor will soon be here,' she added softly. Over the top of Holly's head her eyes met Matt's, and she gave him a tentative smile.

'There are some forms that will require filling out before we can take her down for X Rays,' the nurse said as she carefully examined Holly's arm.

'Mummy, don't leave me!' Holly pleaded as fresh tears formed in her eyes.

Autumn kissed her daughter's forehead. 'Darling, I'll be right back. Matt will stay with you.' She glanced to where Matt was standing on the opposite side of the bed.

'Will you, Uncle Matt?' Holly hiccuped several times.

Matt smiled. 'Of course I will, love.'

'I'll be right back.' Autumn tenderly traced a finger down Holly's tear-stained face before reluctantly following the nurse to the admitting desk.

Four hours later Matt lifted Holly into a cab. Her arm was in a sling, badly bruised but not broken. Autumn had long since told Linc to take Jennifer home, and as the cab driver pulled away from the hospital entrance, Autumn found her glance straying to Matt on the far side of the seat.

Throughout the ordeal he'd held Holly's hand, talked to her, kept her occupied and less fretful. He'd even managed to make Holly laugh, a fact that strangely enough had brought tears to her own eyes.

When the doctor had announced there were no broken bones and that they could take Holly home, Autumn's eyes had filled with tears once more. It was Matt who silently handed her a tissue, and as their glances met, her vision blurred when she saw the tender expression on his face.

Not until they reached the house and Matt was carrying Holly inside did Autumn notice that his limp was even more pronounced. In the confusion she'd forgotten that he, too, was injured.

Autumn and Matt worked together to help Holly undress and get into her nightgown. As Autumn folded her daughter's clothes, she watched Matt gently place a pillow under Holly's arm before tucking the comforter around her.

'You'll feel much better in the morning,' Matt said as he kissed her on the cheek. For a moment he was tempted to lie down beside her. He was exhausted, both mentally and physically. Though he'd managed for the most part to ignore the insistent pain throbbing at his knee, he was beginning to feel the strain.

Autumn's throat tightened with emotion as she watched Matt kiss Holly. Not once during the entire trauma had he been anything but gentle, tender and loving, and not for the first time she found herself thinking what a wonderful father he would make.

She blinked rapidly in an attempt to dispel the tears threatening to fall, and averted her eyes from Matt as he walked slowly toward the door. She crossed to the bed and bent to kiss Holly's flushed cheek. The mild sedative the doctor had administered was taking effect; Holly was almost asleep.

Matt lingered in the doorway, reluctant to leave. He wasn't sure why or what he was waiting for; he only knew that the sight of tears in Autumn's eyes had kept him there.

There had been times during the hours they'd spent at the hospital when he'd wanted to reach out and comfort her. He'd seen the anxiety she'd tried hard to hide.

'She'll be fine. She might even sleep all night. It'll do her good,' Matt said as Autumn walked toward him.

Autumn couldn't speak. There was a huge lump in her throat, and she couldn't for the life of her understand why she should suddenly feel like weeping. As she drew level with Matt, the sob she'd been trying to suppress broke free.

Matt was startled by the sound. Instinctively he reached for her and gently but firmly pulled her into his arms. Her body was soft and warm against his, and as he waited for her tears to subside, he was surprised at how good it felt just to hold her. But as the seconds ticked by the flowery fragrance of her perfume closed around him, awakening a need he could neither contain nor ignore.

When his lips brushed her hair, Autumn's heart stopped in midbeat before it galloped wildly on, sending the blood pounding through her veins. And as his mouth traced a path across her cheek, she was oblivious to everything but the heat spiraling through her.

She was already too close to the flame, already on fire with emotions she'd promised herself never to feel again. And when at last Matt's mouth closed over hers, she felt her heart explode with love.

Matt's pulse kicked into high gear, and a sense of urgency swept through him as he made the discovery that his dreams and memories were indeed a far cry from reality.

What was it about this woman that seemed to draw a response from his very soul? Matt wondered as he found himself floundering in a hot pool of desire. Not until this moment had he realized just how lonely and lost he had been.

Beneath his lips her response was shy, even tentative, reminiscent of that night so long ago, and for a moment Matt thought he was dreaming.

But it wasn't a dream. She was real. Desire, intense and powerful, swamped him once more, and he had to fight to control the need running rampant through him.

Autumn never wanted the moment to end. She'd almost forgotten the sweet ecstasy of being kissed by Matt. As his mouth moved against hers, she marveled at the magical sensations clamoring to life within her. Deeper and deeper he drew her into the mysterious world of desire, but somewhere in a dark corner of her mind a warning bell was ringing.

He had taken her on this trip before, then with a kiss and a promise he'd broken her heart. The memory cooled her blood and brought her quickly to her senses.

Matt was immediately aware of her resistance. He relaxed his hold, knowing that to persist would surely destroy what little chance he might have. Reluctantly he dropped his arms to his sides, and for several minutes they simply stood in silence.

Autumn trembled inside and out, fighting to regain control of emotions she couldn't allow herself to feel. What was it about Matt that aroused such depth of emotion, such overwhelming need, sending all her firm resolutions scattering like leaves in the wind?

Her first instinct was to run to the fragile sanctuary of her room, but even as she began to move away, Matt's voice and words stopped her.

'I'm sorry,' he said, the quiet depth of his tone echoing with sincerity. 'Forgive me. I think we're both a little overwrought. It's been a rather traumatic day, one way or another.' Awkwardly he took a step back, as if to reassure her. The action, however, brought a moan to his lips.

The tension between them evaporated as concern for Matt overrode her need to flee. 'Is it your knee?' she asked.

'Yes.'

'You should lie down and put an ice pack on it,' she suggested.

'You're probably right, but first things first. I think I'll make myself a little more presentable before I venture downstairs. I don't know about you, but I'm starved.'

A quiet rumbling sound coming from his midsection followed this declaration, and with a quick glance at Matt, Autumn couldn't stop the smile tugging at the corners of her mouth.

The smile took his breath away, and Matt had to curb the sudden urge to pull her back into his arms.

'I hear what you mean,' she said, laughter rumbling in her throat now at the rather comical expression on his face. 'I think I'll freshen up a little, too,' she added, turning toward her bedroom door.

'I'll see you downstairs in a few minutes,' Matt said as he limped away.

Once in her own room, Autumn crossed the floor and entered the bathroom. She ran a little water in the sink and slowly, thoughtfully, she unbuttoned her blouse and removed it. Glancing at her reflection in the mirror, she was surprised to see the wistful expression of longing on her face.

Sighing, she closed her eyes, and instantly those moments when Matt had kissed her flashed into her mind. With that one kiss Matt had effectively swept away the barriers she'd built around her heart, forcing her to admit that her feelings for him were very much alive and as potent as they'd been five years ago. She bent and gently splashed her face, wishing it was as easy to wash away the emotions churning inside her.

Matt had made love to her five years ago and on that alone she'd believed he must be in love with her. How naive she had been.

That there was still a spark of attraction between them was evident in the kiss they'd shared, but she couldn't afford to fill her head with hopes and dreams. Now that he knew Holly was his, it was possible he simply looked upon her as a means to get closer to Holly.

9

Ten minutes later Autumn walked into the kitchen to find Matt and Caroline chatting amiably. As Matt's glance swung to hers, she tried to stifle the response that stirred to life within her.

He had changed from the casual sweatshirt and jeans into a cream silk shirt and black pants, and the effect was quite simply stunning. Her pulse kicked into high gear, and it took a lot of effort to meet his gaze.

'There you are,' Matt said, his tone as smooth as a caress. 'I was just about to come looking for you.' He followed the words with a smile, an action that effectively annihilated the wall she'd been carefully rebuilding around her heart.

She had changed her blouse and brushed out her hair, letting it fall loose around her face, and there was no mistaking the look of approval she could read in his eyes. She swallowed and managed to find her voice. 'I peeked in on Holly. She's fast asleep.'

'She will be all right, won't she?' Mrs. Brady asked, anxiety in her eyes.

'Her arm will hurt for a few days, but she'll be fine,' Autumn assured her, beginning to feel hungry.

'That's a relief,' came the reply. 'Mr. Kingston . . . Matt,' Caroline amended with a smile in his direction, 'told me what happened. Poor little mite.' She was silent for a moment. 'Shall I serve dinner now?' she continued.

'Yes, thanks Caroline,' Autumn said, then turned toward the dining room.

The room, though small, was tastefully decorated. The antique Duncan Phyfe table and chairs and matching buffet had belonged, she knew, to Paul's mother. The light from the chandelier was muted, casting delicate shadows over the scene.

The two place settings on the table seemed strangely intimate to Autumn, and she was tempted to cross to the lamps on either side of the buffet and switch them on.

She curbed the impulse and turned to find Matt lowering himself into one of the dining room chairs.

'Pardon my manners,' he said. 'But I need to sit down,' he added as he gently massaged his left knee.

'That's all right,' Autumn quickly assured him.

Caroline Brady appeared in the doorway carrying a tray of steaming dishes, which she placed on the table. She removed the dishes from the tray, then addressed Autumn.

'I was wondering if it was still all right for me to pop out for a while this evening?'

'Oh, yes! I'd forgotten. You told me this morning you'd made plans to visit your sister tonight,' Autumn said.

'Then you don't mind if I go?' Caroline asked.

'Of course not,' Autumn replied.

'Dessert's on the counter, and the

coffeepot just has to be plugged in,' Caroline told her.

'Thanks. We'll manage. Have a nice evening,' Autumn added as Caroline closed the door behind her.

Autumn crossed to the table and sat down. In silence they served themselves from the dishes Caroline had left.

The tantalizing aroma of chicken and herbs filled her senses, making her mouth water. As Matt handed her the bowl of broccoli, their fingers touched, and at the fleeting contact she felt the familiar jolt of awareness dart along her arm.

Her eyes flew to his, and an electric charge arced between them, leaving her breathless. She dropped her gaze and gave her full attention to the plate of food in front of her. It wasn't fair that he should be sitting there looking so damn attractive, so incredibly male, she thought.

From beneath lowered lashes she stole a glance at him once more, noticing now as she studied his profile that the lighting seemed to have created an atmosphere that was both intimate and romantic.

Matt deliberately focused his attention on his plate, but his thoughts were on Autumn. When she'd walked into the kitchen a few minutes ago, he'd felt as if he'd been kicked by a mule. She'd freed her hair from the confines of the braid, letting it fall in silky waves around her face. And the blouse she wore now was the color of dark sapphires, highlighting the exquisite paleness of her skin and accentuating the blue of her eyes.

He could easily see how any man could become obsessed with her. She was all any man could want in a woman: intelligent, beautiful, exciting and compassionate. Oh, yes, compassionate, he thought, recalling how generously she had acted when Holly had been hurt.

'I wanted to thank you,' he began, suddenly needing to let her know.

She frowned at him, and he had the

strongest urge to lean over and kiss the tiny creases that appeared near her eyes. 'Thank me? For what?' she asked.

'For not blaming me for Holly's accident,' he said, and was warmed by the look of surprised appreciation that flickered in her eyes.

'It wasn't your fault,' she stated evenly.

'Perhaps not, but if I'd been a little more careful it wouldn't have happened.' A shiver danced across his skin as the image of Holly toppling to the ground came into his mind.

'Don't be so hard on yourself,' Autumn said softly.

'Being a father takes some getting used to,' he said, and at his words she was suddenly swamped with feelings of regret.

'I suppose it does,' she said, managing to push the words past the lump in her throat.

'I felt so helpless . . . ' Matt began.

Autumn's hand instinctively reached out to touch his. 'Don't do this to yourself, Matt. Holly's all right,' she said, trying to ignore the warmth sweeping along her arm and through her entire body.

He met her gaze. 'I hope to God I never have to go through that again.'

'Every parent shares that feeling, Matt,' she acknowledged, reluctantly withdrawing her hand. 'But you can't protect a child from everything — accidents happen. I'm sure you didn't make it through childhood without a few scrapes and bruises along the way.' Her tone was lighter now as she attempted to ease his thoughts away from Holly and the accident.

He stared straight ahead for several long seconds, then a smile appeared. 'Now that I think about it, I guess I put my father through the same kind of hell quite a few times.'

'Your father?'

He picked up his fork and stabbed absently at the food on his plate. 'My mother died when I was two,' he explained. He was silent for a moment.

'I have no memory of her at all. My father was a salesman for a sporting goods company, and he had to travel around a lot. I'm not sure how he managed it, but he took me everywhere with him. By the time I started school, he'd opened his own sporting goods store in Prince George.' He stopped and turned to her. 'I'm sorry. You don't really want to hear all this.'

'No . . . please go on,' she prompted. He'd rarely spoken about his childhood that summer five years ago, and because she'd always felt that Holly was so much more like Matt, she was eager to listen and learn a little about the kind of child he had been.

Matt saw the genuine interest reflected in her eyes, and a feeling of contentment washed over him. It felt so right sitting here with Autumn. This was what had been missing from his life — a woman to share the ups and downs of daily life, a woman to love him, a family to come home to.

But he'd walked away from the

promise of all of those things five years ago, believing then that Autumn needed time to grow, to mature. He hadn't given her the chance to make her own decisions, and through his own stupidity he'd lost the only woman he'd ever cared about.

Yes . . . he'd lost her once, but as he gazed across the table at Autumn, he was suddenly, fiercely, determined that he wouldn't lose her again. He'd been given a second chance. He was convinced of that, and now all he had to do was make her believe they could have a life together.

All through dessert, and long after the coffee had grown cold in their cups, Matt talked about some of the scrapes he'd gotten himself into as a child, making her laugh one minute and feel sorry for him the next.

She, in turn, shared some stories of her own childhood, and the sound of his deep, rich laughter filling the room brightened the dark corners of her heart. The hours melted away, and she had to stop from pinching herself to see if she was dreaming.

She found herself thinking that this was what being married to someone would really be like — talking, listening, sharing. With Paul she'd been nothing more than a glorified servant, and until now she hadn't realized how much she'd missed.

Reluctant as she was to break the magical spell that had somehow woven itself around them, she rose and began to clear the dishes from the table. So wrapped up had she been in listening to Matt, she couldn't remember having eaten.

He surprised her by helping her clear everything away, and in a matter of minutes the task was complete. They stood now in the kitchen, and Autumn was the first to break the silence.

'It's late. I'd better look in on Holly,' she said, feeling as awkward as a teenager who'd suddenly found herself alone with the most handsome boy in the class.

'Good idea,' Matt said, and began to limp toward the door.

Autumn stopped. 'Go ahead. I'll catch up. I'll make you that ice pack.'

Matt was about to tell her not to bother, but his knee was once more throbbing painfully. 'Thanks. I'd appreciate that.'

Upstairs in Holly's room, Matt stared down at the sleeping child. She'd managed to kick the covers off, and with a smile he gently tucked her in. Then he turned to find Autumn standing in the doorway, watching him, but as he moved toward her, he couldn't decipher the look that flashed briefly in her eyes. 'Thanks, and good night,' he said softly, taking the ice pack wrapped neatly in a towel from her outstretched hand.

Once in his room, Matt slowly undressed and eased himself onto the bed. He saw at a glance that the swelling around his knee had indeed returned, and with a tired sigh he placed the ice pack on the affected area.

He lay back against the pillows and closed his eyes. It had taken every ounce of self-control not to drop the ice pack on the rug and pull Autumn into his arms. The need to simply hold her had been overpowering, but he'd been afraid such an action would have destroyed the truce they seemed to have reached.

Instead he had to content himself with the memory of the kiss he'd shared with her earlier. He let his thoughts drift back to those moments. The image was so clear in his mind that he could almost taste the sweetness, the innocence . . . He frowned. Her response had been tentative, shy — a reaction more in keeping with a woman with very little experience, certainly not the kind of response he'd have expected from a woman who'd been married for several years.

It was with that thought in his mind that he finally fell asleep.

★　★　★

Matt's eyes flickered open, and to his astonishment he found Holly, dressed in her nightie, her arm in a sling, standing by his bedside. Daylight shone brightly from the window, and he blinked several times, wondering if he was dreaming.

'Are you awake, Uncle Matt?' Holly asked.

The events of the previous afternoon returned, and as he eased himself into a sitting position, his glance told him Holly was looking much better. 'Yes, I'm awake. How's your arm this morning?'

'It still hurts,' she told him gravely. 'Can I ask you something?'

'Of course,' Matt said, then patted the covers beside him. 'Why don't you come up here beside me? Can you manage?'

Holly nodded and climbed awkwardly onto the bed.

'You were a brave young lady yesterday,' Matt said as he waited for her to get comfortable. 'I was very proud of you.'

'You were?'

'You bet! I'm really sorry you were hurt.'

'It wasn't your fault.' Holly's voice wavered as she met his gaze. 'I wanted to wave to Jennifer, so I let go.' Her eyes glistened like bright beacons, and two tears escaped and rolled down her cheeks.

Reaching out, he gently wiped them away. 'Hey, don't cry. Accidents happen. It's over now.' He smiled at her. 'What did you want to ask me?'

Holly sniffed noisily, then her expression changed as she launched into her question. 'Can you come to a special night at the skating rink?'

'What kind of special night is this?' he asked.

'It's just for dads 'cause they don't get to watch their kids skate. Sally said I couldn't go, 'cause I don't have a daddy — ' She stopped, her blue eyes fixed on Matt, her bottom lip quivering. Holly swallowed and hurried on. 'Will you come, Uncle Matt?'

Matt could hardly breathe. He was so overwhelmed with emotion he couldn't speak, but the child before him was waiting expectantly for his answer. 'I'd be honored,' he managed, his voice husky.

'Does that mean you'll come?' Holly's blue eyes sparkled.

'Of course!' His arm went around her carefully, and he leaned over to kiss the top of her head.

Autumn, carrying a breakfast tray for Holly, stood in the doorway, immeasurably moved by the scene she'd just witnessed.

During a long and sleepless night she'd tried in vain to convince herself she didn't care about him, had never cared for him, but she knew she'd only been fooling herself. But loving Matt was a luxury she couldn't afford.

'Mummy! There you are!' Holly wriggled out of Matt's embrace. 'I asked Uncle Matt about the skating night and he said he'd come,' she informed her.

Autumn kept her eyes on Holly. 'I hope you didn't wake him up just to ask him.'

'I was already awake,' Matt said, letting his glance slide over Autumn. The midnight-blue housecoat she wore highlighted the shimmering gold in her hair and defined the paleness of her features. She looked small and vulnerable standing in the doorway, and nothing would have given him more pleasure than to kiss away the strain he could see etched on her face.

'I brought you breakfast, Holly. How's your arm this morning, darling?' Autumn asked, trying to appear relaxed when, in fact, it was becoming increasingly difficult to keep her eyes on Holly.

'It still hurts a little, but it's okay,' Holly answered. 'I put the sling on by myself,' she told her mother proudly.

'Good for you. Now why don't you hop back into your own bed and eat this,' Autumn said, motioning with her head to the tray.

'I'm hungry. Are you hungry, Uncle

Matt?' Holly turned to him once more.

'Starving,' Matt said, but glancing at Autumn still standing in the doorway, he wasn't altogether sure the hunger he felt at that moment had anything to do with food.

The brief flash of emotion that Autumn saw in Matt's eyes sent heat across her skin. Her gaze was drawn to the smattering of dark hair that covered his chest, and her pulse gathered speed like a stone rolling down a mountain-side.

The dishes on the tray began to tremble slightly, and she tightened her hold in an attempt to keep it steady. Dragging her gaze away from Matt, she said. 'Let's go, Holly. Matt probably wants to get up.'

'That's okay. She can eat it in here if she wants,' Matt said, reluctant to let either of them leave.

'Can I, Mom?' Holly asked eagerly, obviously enjoying the attention being showered on her.

Autumn checked the impulse to

order Holly back to her own room. 'Okay,' she said as she moved toward the bed, all too aware of Matt's blue eyes watching her. She held the tray toward him, and as they made the transfer, his fingers accidentally brushed hers. For a distressing second she thought she was going to drop everything.

'I've got it,' Matt said, and as he relieved her of the tray, it was all she could do not to turn and run.

'Thank you, Mummy,' Holly said sweetly as she reached for the glass of orange juice.

'I'll leave you to it. I have to get ready for work . . . ' She turned to make her escape.

'Am I going to play school today?' Holly asked, causing Autumn to halt.

Autumn turned to face them once more. 'I think you should stay home for a day or two,' she said evenly.

'Okay,' came the reply.

Autumn smiled, glad that Holly hadn't argued the point. Once back in her room, she let out a silent sigh of relief. Her skin still tingled where Matt had touched her, and she hoped he hadn't noticed her reaction.

The memory of all that had taken place last night, the hours spent over dinner, and the kiss — how could she ever forget that kiss? — had unlocked the door to emotions, hopes and dreams she'd thought safely buried, leaving her feeling fragile and very vulnerable. She needed time to rebuild defenses that had started to crumble almost from the moment he'd arrived.

Twenty minutes later she emerged from her room wearing her white nurse's uniform. The door to Matt's room was closed, and she immediately crossed the hall to find Holly propped up in her bed, browsing through one of the large picture books from her supply on the nearby shelf.

'Mrs. Brady will be up to check on you. You don't have to stay in bed all day, unless you want to,' Autumn said as she sat down on the bed. 'I'll be home after lunch. Will you be all right till then?'

Holly nodded and smiled.

'Oh, by the way, Uncle Linc called earlier to ask how you were, and Jennifer said to say hello and hopes to see you soon.'

'Uncle Matt's going out, too,' Holly said, closing the book with a thump.

'But I'll be back before you know it,' Matt said from the doorway. He was wearing gray slacks, a pale yellow shirt, and over his shoulders hung a dark green wool sweater, its sleeves tied in a loose knot across his chest. His hair was still damp from the shower, and his clean-shaven face looked strong, smooth and inviting. The tangy fragrance of wood and lime drifted toward her, creating a longing she could neither ignore nor deny.

'Where are you going, Uncle Matt?' Holly asked, effectively cutting through the tension.

'I'm going to the clinic, too. I was hoping I might catch a ride with your mother. Dr. Scott's going to take a look at my knee,' he explained.

'Does it still hurt?' Holly asked.

'Yes. But just a little,' he added when he saw her glance worriedly at his leg. 'My appointment's at nine. Would you mind if I tagged along?' he asked Autumn, thinking how smart and efficient she looked in the trim white nurse's uniform, and remembering with a pang that she'd been wearing a similar uniform the evening he'd first waited for her outside the hospital.

But gone was the youthful eagerness he'd found so appealing, and in its place was a maturity, a haunting beauty and a sensuality that caught at his heart and tied him in knots.

'By all means,' Autumn said, thankful that the clinic was only ten minutes away. 'See you later, darling,' she added as she kissed Holly.

The journey to the clinic was completed in total silence. Matt appeared preoccupied, and Autumn was content not to engage in conversation. She parked the car in her allotted space at the rear of the building and together they made their way to the entrance.

'Dr. Scott's office is down the hall and to the left,' she told him, coming to a halt inside the front doors.

'I'll find it,' Matt replied absently, making no move to leave.

She studied him for a moment, noticing the lines of tension on his face as well as the look of anxiety in his eyes. Instinctively her hand moved to touch his arm in a gesture meant solely to comfort. 'Don't worry, Matt. David Scott is one of the best doctors in the field of sports medicine. You're in good hands. He'll have you back on the ice in no time.'

Matt stared uncomprehendingly at her for a long moment before he realized what she was talking about. His mind was still back at the house, with Holly. Throughout the short journey to the clinic, he'd been pondering how he could ensure a place for himself in the lives of Autumn and

Holly and in their futures.

'That's what I'm afraid of,' he said softly. If he was back on the ice, it would also mean he'd be back in Toronto — three thousand miles from Holly and Autumn. And for the first time in his life he found himself wishing he'd chosen a different career.

He smiled when he saw the puzzled frown on Autumn's face. His hand came up to gently trace a path across her cheek. 'I'll see you later,' he said before turning and moving off in the direction she'd indicated.

Autumn stood transfixed as she watched Matt move away. Not until he was out of sight did she release the breath trapped in her lungs. With fingers that were trembling she brought her hand to her cheek.

The sound of the elevator doors opening behind her brought her out of her reverie, but as she rode to the fourth floor her thoughts lingered on Matt.

What was the harm in admitting that

she liked him a little, admired him a little? Not many men would have reacted positively on learning they had a four-year-old daughter. The anger and outrage she'd seen at first had been replaced by a loving acceptance of the child, and she knew he couldn't have found a better way to her heart if he'd tried.

He'd agreed to attend the special skating night with Holly, and suddenly Autumn found herself wanting to believe that he wouldn't hurt the child, wouldn't let her down.

But could she trust him? Matt's life — his hockey career — was in Toronto, and in all probability he would be returning there in the not too distant future. She would do well to remember that.

10

'Then I'll require surgery,' Matt said as he followed David Scott from the examination room into his office.

'Yes, you will,' David confirmed. 'There's a tear of your medial meniscus, and I'm certain you have a loose piece of cartilage floating around in there. It means you'll require arthroscopic surgery, a fairly common procedure now, and it will eliminate the pain and swelling you're experiencing.'

'I see,' Matt said. 'And the prognosis?'

'I'll be able to tell you better after the surgery,' David said, dropping Matt's file onto his desk. 'It's unfortunate that it's the same leg you broke earlier this year.'

'Is that a factor?'

'Most definitely,' David replied as he lowered himself into the leather chair behind the desk. 'All in all, your leg's taken quite a beating. Though injuries are a way of life for hockey players, the more damage you sustain and the older you get, the tougher it is to bounce back.' He stopped to stroke his chin, then glancing across at Matt, he continued. 'I think — but it's only my opinion, mind you — that the original break merely compounded your risk of getting injured. Tell me, how did your leg feel when you went back on the ice?'

'Good, but not great,' Matt said. After four months of hospital visits and therapy, he'd been impatient to get back into the swing of things. His leg had bothered him a little at first, and he'd noticed that he had to rest it more frequently, but he'd persevered.

'It may be that you returned too soon,' David commented, then glanced down at the file on his desk. 'You're how old now?'

'Thirty,' Matt said. 'Are you trying to tell me I'm getting too old for this game?' he asked with a chuckle.

The doctor smiled. 'Could be. But seriously, Matt, you'll need extensive therapy afterward, either here at the clinic or with a therapist in Toronto.' He frowned. 'You weren't expecting to rejoin the team in Europe?'

'No. The tour's finished. When you get through with me here, I'll be heading back to Toronto,' Matt explained. 'So, when can you do the surgery?'

David picked up a notebook from the desk and carefully scanned it. 'How about three o'clock Friday afternoon?'

★   ★   ★

It was five-thirty on Friday afternoon when Autumn, still in her uniform, stepped from the elevator and made her way down the corridor to Matt's private room on the third floor. She'd just completed her shift and should have been on her way home, but had promised Holly she'd pop in and see how Matt was doing.

He'd only been back from the

operating room less than an hour, and she knew he'd still be a little drowsy, but she told herself she wouldn't stay long. She stopped outside his room, and taking a deep, steadying breath, tapped softly on the door, then slipped noiselessly inside.

At the sight of Matt lying in bed, his eyes closed, his broad shoulders encased in a pale blue hospital gown, a strange sensation curled in the pit of her stomach. He looked utterly defenseless and very vulnerable, and she stood motionless, drinking in his finely chiseled features. His hair was in soft disarray, and as she gazed at him she found herself wishing she could soothe away the lines of strain creasing his brow.

Several dark curls had fallen onto his forehead, giving him a youthful, almost boyish appearance, and not for the first time she wondered at the havoc he caused in her heart and to her senses.

She knew she should leave before he opened his eyes and found her there but as if drawn by a magnet, she silently moved toward the bed, her thoughts skimming over the past four magical days.

During that time she'd come to know a side of Matt she hadn't realized existed. He had been an attentive and loving uncle to Holly, playing with her, listening to her, laughing with her — purely and simply enjoying his daughter, loving her as Paul had never done.

It had been like something out of a dream — a dream, she had to keep reminding herself, that wouldn't, couldn't, last.

She knew she should have tried to curtail the time Holly spent with Matt, but that had been easier said than done. Holly had blossomed under the love and attention he'd bestowed on her, and watching them together, Autumn had found it increasingly difficult to keep her own emotions under wraps.

Each night she'd tossed and turned, fighting with her conscience and her fears. She should have been trying to protect Holly, preparing her for Matt's eventual departure from their lives, but somehow she, too, had fallen under his spell.

It was distressing enough to face the knowledge that Holly would be heart-broken when he left, but the realization that her own heart was in grave danger of being similarly affected had rocked her to the core.

She blinked back the tears suddenly threatening to fall and silently gazed down at the figure on the bed.

Matt sighed. The mild sedative he'd been given to help him relax during the surgery was beginning to wear off. Images of Autumn and Holly had been floating in and out of his mind, and he could almost swear he could smell a hint of the fragrance Autumn always wore.

During the past few days he'd learned a lot about what it meant to be a father. He'd learned the joy only a child could bring. And the warmth, the love, and laughter they'd shared had affected him in ways he hadn't dreamed possible. He felt a sense of belonging, a sense of having come home, and he was at a loss to know how to hold on to the treasure he'd found.

He'd come to realize that something vital had been missing from his life, and each moment he spent with Holly and Autumn had shown him all that life could mean — a child, a home, a family.

It came as no surprise to him that he wanted it all. For with each passing day he'd found himself falling more deeply in love with the woman who was the mother of his child.

Though there had been no repetition of the kiss they'd shared that evening outside Holly's bedroom, there had been times during the past few days when he'd only had to look at her and he was gripped by a need so strong that it had taken all his willpower to control it.

He'd spent several sleepless nights,

and in those lonely hours before dawn he'd found himself trying to unravel the mystery that was Autumn, trying to come to terms with the fact that instead of tracking him down, getting word to him about the baby, she had turned to Paul.

Suddenly a strange thought ran through his befuddled brain. Was it possible Autumn had gone to Paul in the hope that Paul might be able to tell her how to get in touch with him?

Where had that come from? he wondered. Surely in his quest to find an answer, he wasn't desperate enough to think that Paul . . .

A muffled sound broke into this thoughts, and he opened his eyes to see Autumn standing only a few feet away. Matt felt his heart kick against his ribs in reaction, and an all too familiar ache began to settle over him. How he wished he could wake up every day and find her at his side. The thought made him smile.

'Hello,' he said softly.

'Hello,' she managed. 'How are you?'

'I'm fine, I think,' Matt said, and began to ease himself into a more comfortable position.

Autumn automatically approached the bed, and picking up a loose pillow, she shook it gently before placing it behind Matt's head. It was a natural action, one any nurse would have carried out for a patient, but Matt was no ordinary patient, no ordinary man.

Her heart shuddered to a standstill, and the air in her lungs seemed to freeze when she realized exactly how close she was to him. Her eyes flew to his, and as their glances collided, the spark of tension suddenly crackling between them could have ignited a bonfire.

Mesmerized by the look in his eyes, she found she lacked the strength to move away. And when his hand came up to brush aside a tendril of hair that had escaped from the confines of her nurse's cap, her heart began to skip and jump like a lamb in a field of clover.

She was suddenly filled with a longing to touch him, to taste him, to know again the glorious sensations only he could arouse. When his hand cupped her head and gently urged her closer, she was incapable of denying herself what she'd been dreaming about and aching for.

When his lips at last touched hers, they were soft and warm and there was a beguiling sweetness in their caress. With delicate, feather-light kisses he teased and tantalized until she thought she would faint from the need building inside her.

When the tip of his tongue touched the moist curve of her upper lip, a shudder ran through her, and her mouth opened in a silent gasp of wonder. One by one her senses were springing to life, and as his mouth grew more urgent, more demanding, the heat spiraling through her was deliciously familiar and all she remembered it to be.

But suddenly the memory of the

night he'd made love to her washed over her, bring with it a cold splash of reality. She had given Matt her trust and her love once before, and he had taken all she had offered and disappeared, leaving her alone and devastated.

'No!' The word was torn from her, and as she broke free from Matt's embrace, she saw a flash of frustration, and something else in the depths of his eyes.

Matt almost groaned aloud in protest as Autumn pulled away. From the first moment his mouth touched hers he'd been aware of her timid response. But as the kiss grew in intensity and her response soared to match his, all thought of restraint had flown out the window. She had wanted him. There had been no doubt in his mind. So why had she pulled away? And had that been fear he'd glimpsed in her eyes? But what was she afraid of?

A knock shattered the tense silence, startling them both. The door swung open, and their glances turned toward the newcomer.

The man in the doorway hesitated, as if sensing something was wrong. 'I'm sorry. The nurse at the desk told me it was all right.'

'Stan! Come on in.' Matt beckoned to his friend. 'I didn't think I'd be seeing you again so soon.'

'If you'll excuse me, I was just leaving,' Autumn interrupted, moving toward the door, and before either man could speak, she was gone.

Autumn didn't stop until she reached the sanctuary of her car. She sat for several minutes slumped behind the wheel, waiting for the storm raging inside her to subside.

The memory of Matt's kiss had stirred up a hornet's nest of memories and emotions, and she had to bite down on her lower lip to suppress the tears threatening to fall.

She wouldn't cry. Damn him! She'd cried enough tears over him. All he'd ever brought her was pain and heartache. No. That wasn't strictly true. He had given her the most precious gift of all — Holly . . .

Holly! Dear heaven! Autumn sat upright and fumbled for the keys in the pocket of her uniform. She started the engine and deftly maneuvered the car from the parking spot.

But as she turned into the stream of traffic, she found her thoughts suddenly twisting in a totally different direction. Where would she be now, she wondered, if she hadn't agreed to Paul's proposal? It was a question she'd asked herself a hundred times.

Though he had cleverly manipulated her into a marriage that was no marriage at all, at the time her options had been limited. The well-being of the child she'd been carrying had been her only thought.

Autumn's fingers tightened on the steering wheel, and a pain began to throb at her temples. Paul had indeed been a troubled young man, but he'd made it possible for her to keep the baby, and for that she would always be grateful.

On reflection she saw now that a major part of Paul's problem had simply been a lack a maturity. He'd wanted — no, expected — immediate success and widespread recognition as an artist, and while his early paintings had shown the promise of genius and received favorable reviews, he hadn't become a celebrity overnight.

The fact that Matt's success and rise to stardom appeared to have happened quickly had possibly fired Paul's jealousy and resentment toward his step-brother. But what Paul had conveniently forgotten was the fact that Matt's success hadn't happened overnight, that, in fact, he'd spent years working hard in the pursuit of his goal.

Learning he had leukemia had sent Paul into the depths of despair, a fact she had seen for herself, but the knowledge that he was dying had obviously fueled his anger and distorted his thinking.

It was ironic and more than a little sad that since his death Paul's paintings were receiving the acclaim he'd yearned for throughout his life. While he may have lacked a certain maturity, and the motive behind his offer of marriage had stemmed from a twisted kind of revenge, she suddenly found herself willing and able to forgive and forget.

For the first time Autumn saw Paul's actions in a new light. Perhaps he had actually saved her and Matt from a marriage that, given the circumstances, might have ended in disaster.

She'd told herself numerous times that even if Matt had known about the baby, there had always been the question of whether or not he would have accepted responsibility for the child. Theirs had been a summer romance — a passionate encounter — and during the few weeks they'd been seeing each other, Matt had never once spoken about love, or commitment.

His hockey career had been an important part of his life then, as it was now, and if he had asked her to marry him, she would have been the one expected to make all the sacrifices. She would have had to uproot herself, relocate to another town.

Having to adjust to a husband, a child, and a way of life she knew nothing about wouldn't have been easy. Marriage was at best a gamble, and theirs would have started out on rather shaky ground, with Matt possibly resenting the choice he'd been forced to make.

But that had no bearing on the problem facing her now. As Holly's natural father, Matt did have rights, but he'd made no requests, no demands — yet. He cared about Holly. That much was evident. He'd shown it in every conceivable way. And even now she was surprised at the feeling of jealousy that crept into her heart.

How could she fault him? He was simply getting to know his daughter, but it seemed to Autumn that during the past few days he'd been as charming and attentive to her as he'd been to Holly. She'd found herself wanting to trust him, wanting to accept the friendship he seemed to be offering.

Her heart skipped a beat as a fierce yet familiar longing assailed her. She wanted more than friendship; she wanted it all. Angrily she now chastised herself for forgetting the pain and disillusionment she'd suffered at his hands five years ago.

A sob rose in her throat and she fought to suppress it. Since Matt's return to Vancouver, she'd had to constantly fight to keep her feelings under control.

She tried to tell herself that she'd be relieved — no, glad — when Matt returned to Toronto, but she knew she was lying. With each encounter, each kiss, he had successfully chipped away the wall she'd built around her emotions.

Her foolish heart had refused to heed all her warnings, welcoming back with joy the only man she'd ever wanted, the only man she'd ever loved.

11

'He's here! Uncle Matt's here!' It was Saturday, and Holly's excited cry brought Autumn from the kitchen where she'd been talking to Caroline Brady.

He'd telephoned earlier to say he was being released from the clinic, but when she made the polite offer to collect him, he'd thanked her and told her he'd already made arrangements. Then, in a soft yet ominous tone, he'd added that there were things they needed to discuss. Just as solemnly she'd agreed, but as she hung up the phone she hadn't been able to stop her hands from shaking.

'Careful, pumpkin, or you'll have us both on the floor.' She heard the deep, familiar voice moments before the front door swung open to reveal Matt dressed in gray slacks with a navy sweater over a blue open-necked shirt. He was balancing precariously between a pair of crutches while Holly danced at his side.

'Watch out, darling,' Autumn cautioned Holly, afraid as Matt had been that the child would somehow become entangled in the wooden supports.

Matt's gaze lifted to meet hers, and he found himself wishing the endearment had been for him. He noticed the faint blush that tinged her cheeks, and noted too that her eyes appeared almost as bright as the turquoise dress she wore. She looked wonderful, and he marveled at the effect she had on him.

He held her gaze, but only for a second, and in that moment he saw a flash of heat flicker briefly in the depth of her eyes, causing that now familiar ache to spread through him.

'Hi,' he said, wondering a little at the breathless tone in his voice.

'Can I try your crutches?' Holly asked. Not without a little reluctance, Matt brought his gaze back to the child by his side.

He smiled down at her. 'I'm using them at the moment,' he said.

'They're too big for you anyway,' Autumn pointed out, 'and I don't think it's a very good idea for you to try them.'

'But, Mom!' Holly began.

'Darling, Matt needs those crutches to get around, and besides,' Autumn continued, 'you might hurt yourself.'

'Your mother's right,' Matt acknowledged before Holly could protest further. 'We don't want to be running you to the hospital again, do we? Besides, who would carry you out to the car?'

Holly giggled. 'Oh, Uncle Matt. You are silly.'

Autumn threw a grateful glance at Matt, noting the lines of pain and fatigue around his mouth. 'I think Matt might like to sit down,' she suggested.

'Thanks, I would,' Matt agreed, warmed by the concern he could see on her face.

'Holly, run and tell Mrs. Brady we'll

have lunch in the living room. Then go upstairs and finish putting away your toys. I told you no lunch until you do, remember?'

'Do I have to?' Holly asked, looking pleadingly at her mother.

'Yes, young lady, you have to,' Autumn responded.

Holly sighed. 'Okay,' she said, obviously sensing that the battle was lost. With a shrug of her small shoulders she smiled at Matt before scampering off.

Autumn moved to close the front door, and as she did so the telephone started to ring.

'My bag is outside on the steps,' Matt said. 'The taxi driver put it there for me,' he added as he swung himself rather awkwardly toward the living room.

Autumn stepped outside and picked up the small overnight bag. Closing the front door, she dropped his bag at the foot of the stairs and joined Matt in the living room.

She found him standing beside the

love seat, his expression serious, and instinctively Autumn knew the talk he had mentioned earlier on the telephone was about to begin.

'There are some things we need to discuss,' Matt began, but before he could continue there was a knock at the door.

Caroline Brady entered, an anxious look on her face. 'Excuse me, Mrs. Daniels, Mr. Kingston.'

'Yes, Caroline?' Autumn said, not sure whether to be relieved at the interruption.

'That was a reporter from the local newspaper on the telephone. He asked if you were here, Mr. Kingston, and I said yes. Then he asked me if it was true you'd had an operation on your knee. I said I didn't know anything about an operation and I hung up.' She looked from one to the other.

'That's fine, Mrs. Brady. You did the right thing,' Matt assured her. 'Thank you.'

'Damn!' Matt muttered the moment

Mrs. Brady was out of earshot. 'I guess it was wishful thinking on my part to hope I'd have a few more days of peace and quiet before the press got hold of the story.'

'How could they have found out?' Autumn asked.

'Oh, any number of ways,' Matt said. 'By rights, I should be at training camp. It was no secret that I'd been injured, and it wouldn't take much for a smart reporter to put two and two together.' He'd barely finished talking when the telephone rang once more. Their gazes locked for a second.

'Shall I answer it this time?' Autumn asked, moving to the table near the bar.

'Yes, but don't say anything,' he instructed.

'And just how do you propose I do that?' Autumn asked, unable to stop herself from smiling.

Matt stared uncomprehendingly at her for a moment, then he began to laugh. Autumn joined in and for several seconds they were caught in the magic of a shared moment.

Caroline stood in the doorway once again. 'I'm sorry to bother you again. This time the caller says he's from a local radio station. I thought I'd better ask what I should do. He wants to talk to you.'

'I bet,' Matt said, all signs of laughter quickly disappearing from his face. 'Tell him I'm unavailable and hang up. And, Caroline, it might be a good idea to take the phone off the hook for a while.'

The housekeeper turned her gaze on Autumn, and she readily nodded her assent.

'It looks like we might be in for a siege,' he said, a frown on his face. 'But that's not important at the moment. Right now I want to talk about Holly.' He made a move, adjusting his stance, and as a result the crutches wobbled. Instinctively Autumn reached out to steady him, then stopped. Clasping her arms about her, she prepared herself for what was to come.

Matt cursed under his breath as he

regained his balance. 'It won't surprise you, I'm sure,' he said, his eyes on Autumn, 'when I say that I want to be a part of Holly's future. I may be rather new at being a father, but I want to learn. I want to be there for her when she needs me.'

Autumn clamped her teeth together, fighting as always to hold back emotions suddenly threatening to overwhelm her. She remained silent, wishing Matt would finish what he'd started. Holly might come rushing in at any moment, and this was one conversation she didn't want the child to hear.

'I've done a lot of thinking about this,' Matt continued. 'There seems to be only one solution that I can see.' He stopped, and Autumn met his gaze head-on. 'What I'm trying to say is that I think it's in Holly's best interests that we get married.'

Autumn's mouth dropped open, and she stared at Matt in utter disbelief. She felt as if someone had suddenly landed a punch in her midsection.

Of all the things she'd expected him to say, of all the suggestions he might have made concerning visiting rights and privileges, marriage hadn't even been on the chart. Marriage! She was still reeling from the shock.

'I know this might come as a surprise to you,' Matt went on, 'but I believe it's the only fair solution.' He swung the crutches and moved closer, as if by doing so he would better be able to convey his true feelings.

He wanted to marry her because he loved her — had always loved her — and during the past week he'd come to realize that his life would be nothing without her, or Holly. The idea of marriage had popped into his head only seconds after she'd fled from his hospital room. And while he knew he was being selfish, wanting it all, the more he'd thought about it the more he'd begun to believe he could make it work.

And once they were married — he refused at the moment to consider that she might reject his suggestion — he could then try to break down the barriers she had erected. Perhaps then he might uncover the answers to some of the questions puzzling him. But he was willing to forget the past and fight for a chance at happiness.

'Is this some kind of joke?' Autumn asked, finding her voice at last.

'Dammit, Autumn, it's no joke.' His tone held anger and impatience as he went on. 'I've already missed some of the most important years of Holly's life and I don't intend to miss any more. Eventually, of course, I think she should be told the truth. We can do that together . . . ' He reached out as if to touch her. 'We could make it work . . . for Holly's sake.'

At this last plea Autumn twisted away, biting down hard on her lip. Matt was asking her to marry him, but the offer was out of love for Holly and nothing more. Dear God! If only he loved her, too. She felt a hysterical giggle begin to surface and she fought it down. But it was laughable. Paul had offered her marriage without love, and she'd found herself in a situation full of hate and revenge. Was Matt's offer really any different?

In the dark, secret corner of her heart she wanted to shout, 'Yes, I'll marry you,' because she loved him and the thought of becoming his wife, for whatever reason, was like being granted a wish. But she wasn't Cinderella, and there was no fairy godmother with a magic wand waiting in the wings. He was asking her to be his wife, to trust him, to accept him as Holly's father. But if she agreed to marry him, she knew she would be leaving herself open to the kind of heartache that might eventually destroy her. Deep inside, pain began to vibrate through her.

'I cleaned up my room, Mummy,' Holly said suddenly, her voice breaking through the silence. 'I'm starving. Is lunch ready?' She glanced from one adult to the other, then a frown puckered her brow. 'Mummy . . . ?'

Holly's voice quivered slightly, and instantly Autumn crossed to the child, scooped her into her arms and hugged her tightly.

'Yes, lunch is ready,' she said, kissing Holly's forehead. 'See? Here's Mrs. Brady,' she added, setting Holly, who was smiling now, back on the floor.

Caroline Brady, carrying a tray of dishes, some with sandwiches and some with cakes, joined them and placed the tray on the coffee table in front of Matt. The tension in the room had all but dissipated now, but the turmoil raging inside Autumn was like nothing she'd ever known before.

Holly grinned at Autumn, her anxiety forgotten. 'I like egg sandwiches best,' she said, reaching for one, and after taking an enormous bite she turned to Matt. 'Whunt shum . . . ?'

Matt couldn't stop the smile curling at the corners of this mouth. 'I think I'll get my own,' he said as he sat down on the love seat beside Holly. 'Thanks,' he added as Mrs. Brady handed him a plate.

'I need to wash up. I'll be right back,' Autumn mumbled, hurrying from the room.

Matt watched her departing figure with a thoughtful frown. He'd made a mess of the proposal. He hadn't meant to sound so . . . mercenary. There had been nothing romantic about his words, no declaration of love, but the fact that she hadn't immediately dismissed his suggestion that they get married was encouraging. He'd shocked her, of that there had been no doubt, but as she stood listening to him, a look he hadn't been able to define had come and gone in her eyes.

His glance slid to Holly who was happily munching on a sandwich. He smiled. At least he wouldn't have to win her over to the idea of accepting him as a new father.

Suddenly he found himself wondering if Holly missed Paul. She rarely talked about him, but perhaps that was a child's normal reaction after the loss of a parent. On the other hand, Holly might simply be taking her cue from Autumn — she didn't talk much about Paul, either.

★ ★ ★

Upstairs in her room, Autumn crossed to the window. She felt trapped in both a physical and emotional sense. Trapped by a set of circumstances over which she seemed to have no control — and trapped by her own treacherous feelings for Matt.

What should she do? Marry him? She'd never considered herself impulsive. She had always been the kind of person who thought things through carefully . . . until Matt had come into her life. She'd fallen head over heels in love with him almost from the moment she'd set eyes on him. But right now she needed to think — to at least try to be objective, to calmly go over the positive and negative aspects of the decision that faced her.

It was obvious Matt wanted the

marriage simply as a means of gaining unlimited access to Holly. He loved the child; it was a fact she couldn't dispute.

Autumn watched a raindrop slide down the windowpane, and felt a tear slip from beneath her lashes and trace a path down her cheek. If she agreed to Matt's proposal, she would be marrying the man she loved, and the father of her child — what more did she want?

So what was her answer going to be? Her heart was strongly in favor of the marriage, and for her own peace of mind she wanted desperately to believe that simply being a part of Matt's life would be enough. But deep in her soul she knew it would never be enough. She wanted his love.

Autumn heard the chimes of the front door, and taking only a moment to wipe the moisture from her face, she made her way downstairs.

The sound of voices barking out questions reached her, and she ran the remainder of the way, immediately realizing that there were reporters at the door. Microphones and small hand-held tape recorders were being thrust in Caroline's face, and the housekeeper was having difficulty keeping the door from swinging wide open.

'I'm sorry. Mr. Kingston isn't available,' Caroline said, her voice edged with panic.

Autumn moved to the housekeeper's side. 'Can I help you, gentlemen?' she asked.

Immediately she was met with a cacophony of noise as the eight people on the doorstep each asked a different question.

'Please. How am I supposed to answer any questions when I can't even hear them?' she almost had to shout.

The noise subsided, but only minimally, and focusing her attention on the young man directly in front of her, she listened to him.

'We're trying to locate Matt Kingston. Is he still a guest in your house?' the reporter asked politely.

The noise level dropped appreciably

as the rest waited for her answer. 'Matt is staying here — ' She got no further, as once again a barrage of questions came flying at her.

She held up her hands and was thankful when the small bevy of reporters grew silent. 'Please, let me finish. Matt is here, but he isn't available at the moment. Now I'd appreciate it very much if you would please leave.'

'Mr. Kingston was seen leaving the David Scott Sports Clinic. Could you tell us if the reason he visited the clinic was because of the injury he sustained in Europe?' The question came from someone at the back of the group.

'I'm sorry, that's a question you'd have to ask Mr. Kingston.' Her calm, matter-of-fact answer effectively silenced the group, and she took the opportunity to close the door.

She turned to Caroline. 'Is the phone still off the hook?'

'Yes.'

'Good!' she said as she turned toward

the living room. She opened the door and almost collided with Matt who, she guessed, had been eavesdropping. Her hand brushed his arm, and she withdrew it immediately, but not before she'd seen a flame flicker in his eyes. She moved past him, wishing she could control her reaction, yet knowing where Matt was concerned it was impossible.

'Do you think they'll be back?' she asked, thankful she managed to keep the tremor from her voice.

'It's possible,' Matt said. 'But at the very least you've given me the breathing space I needed. Thanks. Oh, by the way,' he hurried on, 'Holly asked if she could watch TV for a while. I told her it was all right, but I wasn't sure you even owned one. Where do you hide it?' He swung himself toward the bar, and leaning the crutches against it he reached for a glass.

'There's a TV in Paul's room,' Autumn said automatically. 'He was the only one who ever watched it.'

'Paul's room?' Matt repeated, a

frown on his face. 'You must mean his studio . . . downstairs.'

Autumn made no reply, then turned from Matt's puzzled gaze, silently cursing herself for the slip. Paul's studio was in the basement, but the room he'd slept in, lived in, was on the main floor, at the rear of the house. Autumn's and Holly's rooms were on the second floor, a section of the house Paul had rarely visited.

'But I thought Paul didn't like distractions when he was painting. He was quite adamant about it,' Matt said, his eyes on Autumn, wondering why she suddenly seemed tense and edgy.

Autumn felt her mouth go dry. What could she say? He was right, but to acknowledge that fact would incite more questions, questions she didn't want to answer. She swallowed.

'I never did get a chance to ask how your knee is. Was the surgery successful?' She knew she was babbling, and with each word Matt's frown deepened.

'Why are you changing the subject?'

Matt put the glass down on the counter. 'You don't like to talk about Paul, do you? Why is that? Ever since I arrived I've practically had to drag out of you anything I wanted to know about Paul. Why? Dammit! Something isn't right here.' Matt grabbed his crutches and swung himself around to the front of the bar.

Autumn's heart hammered wildly. The urge to flee was strong, but she forced herself to remain where she was.

Matt stopped in front of her. Anger and frustration rose like a torrent inside him. 'Talk to me. Tell me about Paul. Tell me why you married him. Dammit, tell me why you didn't even try to track me down and let me know you were pregnant.'

'But I — ' She got no further, for Holly came bursting into the room.

'Uncle Matt! Uncle Matt! You're on TV.' Her eyes were wide with excitement. 'I just saw you. The man was talking about you and hockey and everything.'

'What?'

'I'll show you. Come on.' Holly urged before turning and running from the room.

With a frustrated glance at Autumn, Matt swung away, and with a speed that amazed her, he disappeared through the open doorway.

Autumn didn't move. Thoughts were spinning furiously in her head. Had she been hearing things? Matt had angrily accused her of not bothering to let him know that she was pregnant. But she had tried to track him down — and when that had met with no success, Paul had offered to get a message to him . . .

Autumn drew a deep breath as the answer dawned. Had Paul misled her about leaving a message for Matt?

But what did it matter if Paul had lied? Even if Matt hadn't been given the message, he had been the one who had walked out of her life, with a kiss and a promise, and nothing in the world could change that.

12

Matt frowned when he caught sight of Holly disappearing into a room at the end of the hallway. It was a room he'd thought was for storage, at least that was how Paul had described it when he'd taken Matt on a brief tour of the house the first time he'd paid them a visit.

He came to a halt now in the doorway, surprised to note that it wasn't a storage room at all. Directly in front of him, angled around a large television set, was a rocker-recliner, an easy chair and a two-seater couch. Holly was seated on the edge of the rocker, her gaze pinned to the television screen where a hockey game appeared to be in progress.

Puzzled, Matt crossed the threshold. His glance swept the large room which appeared to be a sitting room and bedroom combined, for in the corner to his left sat a brass bed, an antique dresser with a matching wardrobe and a night table.

Paul's room. The words popped into his head as he continued his inspection. Not Paul's studio — that was in the basement. And it wasn't a storage area, or even a play room for Holly. No, it was definitely Paul's room. The words danced in his head, refusing to leave.

'You're not on anymore.' Holly's sorrowful tone broke into his thoughts, bringing Matt's attention back to the child. 'I did see you, Uncle Matt. I did,' she insisted, gazing up at him.

'I'm sure you did, pumpkin,' he said soothingly as he came farther into the room. But his mind was on other matters. Why hadn't Paul wanted him to see this room?

He glanced around once more, this time with a more discerning eye. On the wall near the brass bed he noticed a framed copy of a painting by Constable, a gift Paul had received from his mother. It had little monetary value, but Paul had treasured the print along with several others done by Constable, his favorite landscape artist.

Matt continued to scan the room, focusing on the various paintings and prints hanging here and there on the walls. As his glance slid from one to the other, he could almost feel Paul's presence, and a shiver chased down his spine.

'That's you! See, I told you!' Holly shouted excitedly, pointing at the screen.

'What?' Matt frowned, unable for a moment to fathom what was happening.

'I just changed the channel,' Holly explained, 'and now you're there again. See?'

Matt turned and looked at the television screen, more than a little taken aback to see a photograph of himself staring back.

'The man's talking about you,' Holly said.

'... did not return to Toronto. He was in Vancouver last weekend to attend an exhibition of paintings by the late Paul Daniels. Kingston was seen leaving the David Scott Sports Clinic in Vancouver, fueling speculation that the injury he sustained a month ago in Europe is more serious than at first reported. Kingston, whose contract is due for renewal, could not be reached for comment. Coach Charlie Crawford also declined to comment.'

'Thanks, Charlie,' Matt mumbled under his breath. Before leaving the clinic he'd placed two calls to Toronto. One was to Charlie Crawford, the coach, outlining in detail the doctor's comments regarding the operation, as well as his recommendations. The second call had been to his agent, Alistair McFarlane, asking him to set up a meeting with the manager and owner of the hockey club.

'We'll be right back,' the announcer promised and Holly looked at Matt.

'What's spec ... quool ... ?' Holly

frowned over the word.

'Speculation,' Matt said, coming to her aid.

'Yeah!' Holly said, nodding.

'Well, it just means they're guessing, that they don't know for sure,' he explained.

'Guessing? About what?' she asked.

'Whether my knee is hurt or not,' he added.

'But it is, isn't it? You were in the hospital just like me when I hurt my arm,' Holly said.

'That's right. Your arm's all better now, but it's going to take a little longer for my knee to get better,' he explained.

'How long will you have to use those crutches?'

'A few more days, I think.'

'Does it still hurt?' she asked him, her tone anxious.

'Yes,' he answered truthfully. In fact, at the moment he ached all over, especially where the crutches were digging into him. 'I think I'll go upstairs now and lie down for a while.' He glanced past Holly to the television screen where he noticed a young woman skating. 'Look, Holly, a figure skater.'

Holly immediately turned to the television set. 'Oh, boy!' she exclaimed excitedly, her eyes riveted to the screen.

Matt smiled down at Holly, watching in fascination the expression on her cherublike face. Not for the first time he found himself overwhelmed with a feeling of love for her.

'I'll see you later,' he said softly, but Holly was too wrapped up in the activity on the screen to hear him.

There was no sign of Autumn in the outer hallway, and for a moment Matt was tempted to find her. But his uninjured leg was aching now, undoubtedly from the strain of being the only one in use, and so he made his way up the stairs, surprised that the climb wasn't as difficult as he'd anticipated.

Once in his room, he lay down on the bed and closed his eyes. Immediately there came into his mind an image of

Autumn, and he remembered clearly her shocked reaction to his proposal.

Would she agree? he wondered. She had to! He needed her — how he needed her! With that thought he drifted off to sleep.

★ ★ ★

Matt woke with a start. The room was shadowed and for a moment he thought he was still at the clinic. As his eyes grew accustomed to the lighting, he remembered returning to his room and lying down.

He felt grubby and stiff, but the ache in his knee was minimal. Slowly he eased himself off the bed. Picking up his crutches he headed for the bathroom.

His descent, though awkward, was manageable, and as he reached the foot of the stairs, Autumn appeared from the kitchen.

'I was just coming to find you. Dinner's ready,' she said, noticing he looked less strained and more rested than he had in days. 'It's Caroline's night off. I made spaghetti. I hope you don't mind if we eat in the kitchen.'

'That's fine,' Matt said as he swung himself in that direction.

Autumn held the door open for him, and as he moved past, she kept her eyes averted.

Holly looked up from her task of putting napkins at each place setting and smiled a greeting. 'We're having pisgetti,' Holly said as she hopped up onto a chair.

'I love pisgetti,' Matt told her, an echo of laughter rumbling in his voice.

Autumn busied herself serving the meal while Matt set his crutches on the floor and sat down next to Holly. She was more than a little relieved to let Holly fill the silence. The child chattered about the figure skating she'd watched on television earlier. When Autumn joined them at the table, she tried with some difficulty to ignore the warmth and coziness of the scene.

As they were eating dessert, the telephone rang. Matt glanced over at Autumn, surprise evident on his face.

'I used the phone earlier. I thought it would be safe now to hang up,' Autumn said as she pushed her chair from the table and rose to her feet. She reached for the receiver.

'Hello,' she said, then listened for several seconds. 'Yes, just a moment please.' Taking the phone from the counter she stretched the cord to where Matt sat at the table. 'It's for you. A Mr. McFarlane long-distance from Toronto.' The words almost choked in her throat.

'Thanks,' Matt said, taking the receiver from Autumn's hand.

'Help me clear away the dishes, Holly,' Autumn instructed quietly.

'Hello, Alistair,' Matt said, his tone warm and friendly. 'I didn't expect to hear from you so soon. Did you set up the meeting?'

Autumn forced herself to concentrate on the task at hand, but her ears were tuned in to every word.

'What?' Matt's tone was one of annoyance now, and Autumn let her glance drift in his direction. 'They don't want much, do they? All right. Tell them I'll be there — and, yes, I do know what I'm doing. Thanks, Alistair. I'll call the airport and book a flight as soon as I hang up. Goodbye.'

Matt replaced the receiver and cursed under his breath. He hadn't expected Alistair to set up the meeting so soon. Now he found himself wishing he'd held off calling Toronto. But he'd known that his injury had been a cause for concern, especially since his contract was up for renewal. Negotiations had actually begun several months ago, but with his injury everything had changed — in more ways than he'd ever imagined.

His glance slid to Autumn. 'I have to go back to Toronto,' he said. He watched as the blood drained from her face. A look of pain flitted across her features, and was gone instantly, making him wonder if he'd only imagined it.

She swallowed convulsively. 'You mean now ... tonight?' she asked, trying with some difficulty to keep her voice steady.

'Yes. There's a flight that leaves around midnight,' he told her. 'Or there used to be,' he amended. 'I believe it's called the red-eye. Actually, if it's still on the schedule, it's the same flight I took five years ago.'

There was silence for a moment.

'Are you going away, Uncle Matt?' Holly asked from the other side of the kitchen by the dishwasher, where she'd been helping Autumn. Slowly she came into view, her eyes wide and fixed on Matt.

'Yes, Holly, I'm afraid I have to,' Matt said, silently cursing himself for momentarily having forgotten about Holly. 'But don't look so worried,' he went on, holding out his hand to her now. 'I'll be back.'

'You will?' Holly took several steps

toward him, her blue eyes pleading with him to say yes.

'Yes.' Matt smiled and nodded, wanting to convince her.

'But will you be back in time for the special night at my skating class on Thursday?' Holly asked, stopping just out of reach.

'I wouldn't miss it for the world,' he assured her. But still she hesitated.

'Promise?' Holly's voice was a whisper now.

'I promise,' Matt said with total sincerity, and at those words Holly's smile suddenly reappeared like a bright ray of sunshine.

Autumn watched in a cloud of pain and disbelief as Matt drew the child into his arms. He held her tightly against his chest for several long moments. Words of anger and protest trembled on her lips, and she had to bite down on the inner softness of her mouth to stop them from escaping.

That Holly trusted him, loved him, was as plain as the nose on her face.

Autumn wasn't sure why she felt betrayed, but somehow that was the feeling she was experiencing. It wasn't fair that one man could create such havoc in her life.

Matt slowly, reluctantly, released Holly. 'Why don't you run upstairs and wait for me? I want to talk to your mother for a minute, then I have to pack. You can help me if you like.'

Autumn said nothing as Holly slid from Matt's arms and with a fleeting glance at her mother did as she was bid. The moment they were alone, Autumn couldn't contain herself any longer. 'How could you?' she cried.

Matt retrieved his crutches and stood up, staring in fascination as Autumn glared at him, her blue eyes almost black with anger.

'What's wrong? What are you so angry about?'

She drew a ragged breath, unable to believe he didn't know. 'You shouldn't make promises you don't intend to keep.' She almost shouted.

Surprise flashed in the depths of his eyes and then was gone. 'But I do intend to keep my promise.' He came toward her, stopping only inches away. 'What makes you think I won't?'

Autumn could hardly breathe. Matt's nearness was scrambling her senses, diffusing her anger until the heat of that anger kindled a different kind of heat, a heat that left her weak with longing.

Valiantly she clung to the remnants of her control. 'Holly trusts you. If you break that trust, you'll break her heart, just like — ' She bit down furiously on her lip, stopping the telltale words.

She dropped her eyes from Matt's searching gaze, hardly able to believe what she'd almost said. She began to turn away, but Matt's right hand came out to stop her, the sudden movement sending the crutch under his arm onto the floor.

'Just like . . . what?'

His words were a mere whisper, and it took every ounce of her strength to look into his eyes. All she could do was shake her head, and after what seemed like an eternity, he released her.

'I'll be back, Autumn. You won't get rid of me that easily. Besides, I need an answer to my proposal.' His words brought her eyes back to his. 'Holly trusts me. And from the little I've learned about kids this past week, they're not easily fooled. Perhaps you should take a page from her book and have a little faith. She's my daughter. I have no intention of hurting her, or you. Trust me.' His voice and eyes were imploring her now, and for several heart-stopping seconds she found herself wanting desperately to believe him, to trust him.

But before she could speak his hand dropped away, and with a muttered oath he bent to pick up the fallen crutch, giving her all the time she needed to make her escape.

13

The days, the minutes, the hours until Thursday seemed interminable for Autumn. She was thankful for her job, which helped to pass some of the time at least. At the clinic she tried to keep her thoughts on her work, and for the most part she was successful. But continually her mind would conjure up images of Matt, and she'd catch herself staring into space, daydreaming. She was relieved that no one seemed to notice her preoccupation and she chastised herself for behaving like a lovesick adolescent.

Since Matt's departure a strange feeling of emptiness had settled over her. Holly, on the other hand, seemed happy and content, secure in the belief that Matt would return.

She chattered about him at every opportunity, a situation that tried

Autumn's patience to the limit. But as far as Holly was concerned Matt would be back — no ifs, ands or buts about it. He'd promised her he would take her to the skating rink on Thursday night, and she firmly believed he would fulfill his promise.

And though Autumn wanted desperately to trust Matt, the memory of his sudden departure from her life five years ago still haunted her. She trusted him then, believing that the moments they'd shared had happened out of love and not lust, and that she'd held a special place in his heart. But she'd been wrong.

The weather reflected her own feelings as gray clouds blanketed the sky. The insistent drizzle made driving conditions poor, and as Autumn turned the car into the parking lot of the play school to pick up Holly, she suddenly longed for the sunny days of summer. She was a few minutes early and, as she settled back to wait, her thoughts, once again, turned to Matt.

It was Thursday, but as yet there was no sign of Matt, and no word as to whether or not he still intended to arrive.

Holly had been in a state of excitement from the moment she'd awakened that morning. 'Uncle Matt's coming today! Uncle Matt's coming today!' had been the chant throughout breakfast.

There was still time, of course. And she'd been tempted to call the airport and ask the times of the flights arriving from Toronto. But she'd refrained from taking that step, telling herself that her nerves were already stretched to the breaking point. Clock-watching would serve no purpose.

Autumn's glance moved to the door of the building, which had opened. Children began to emerge, and a few moments later Holly opened the passenger door and climbed in. 'Is he here yet?' were her first words, and as Autumn turned to her daughter, she wished with all her heart she could say yes.

'Not yet, darling,' she said, then surprised herself by adding quickly, 'but there's still lots of time.'

Holly happily accepted this answer, and not for the first time Autumn marveled at the child's unwavering trust.

During lunch Holly talked about the evening ahead and explained to Autumn for the hundredth time exactly where she would be in the lineup on the ice. After lunch Autumn insisted Holly take a nap, and though the child argued a little, once tucked into bed, she was soon fast asleep.

Autumn retired to her own room with the intent of taking a short nap, too, but sleep evaded her as it had done all too often of late. She hadn't slept well since Matt's departure, and as a result she felt tired and edgy.

Holly awoke a little later, refreshed and bubbling with excitement, and once again Autumn had to tell her that Matt hadn't arrived. The news was greeted with the comment, 'He'll be here.' But by seven o'clock there was still no sign of Matt.

He could have called, Autumn thought angrily as she ushered a rather subdued Holly out to the car. And as she drove to the rink, it was all she could do not to shout out her anger and frustration.

He'd broken his promise. The words spun like leaves in the wind inside her head. She should never have trusted him. Never have told him about Holly. *Never have fallen in love with him again* . . . . Her thoughts spun faster now, and she had to fight to stop the tears from falling. For Holly's sake she had to try and remain calm and in control.

'Maybe Uncle Matt will be waiting at the rink,' Holly said, breaking the silence.

'Maybe,' she managed to say, and tried bravely to smile encouragingly at Holly before turning back to the business of driving.

Damn you, Matt Kingston! How

could you do this to Holly . . . to me? He wasn't coming back — he'd played her for a fool again. She had managed to banish him from her heart once before, and she would do it again. But what about Holly? How was she supposed to help Holly cope with the pain of disillusionment?

Autumn pulled the car into the parking area adjacent to the rink. It had stopped raining, and Autumn could see a small group of parents standing outside the building. Taking Holly's hand in hers, they made their way toward the front doors.

Just as they reached the door, Autumn heard a shout. 'Autumn! Holly! Wait!'

Holly spun around, her eyes eagerly searching for the owner of the voice. Suddenly her face lit up with a brilliant smile. Tugging her hand free of Autumn's, she ran toward Matt, who was climbing out of a taxi.

'Uncle Matt! Uncle Matt! I knew you'd come,' Holly said as she threw herself into his open arms.

'Hey, slow down!' Matt laughed as he pressed her to him and hugged her as if he would never let go. God, how he had missed her, and Autumn! Where was she? He searched the faces of the people on the sidewalk, looking for her. Since he'd been gone, the days had seemed endless and totally empty. It amazed him how much they had both come to mean to him. 'Where's your mother?' Matt asked as he set Holly back on the ground.

'Right there.' Holly pointed back the way she had come.

Matt scanned the faces once more, and his heart tripped over when he finally caught sight of Autumn standing near the door. She looked pale and a little tired, but beautiful nonetheless, and he let his eyes feast on her for a moment. He wanted nothing more than to close the gap between them and take her in his arms. But he checked the impulse.

Autumn felt her heart jump as her

eyes locked with Matt's. He had come! He had kept his promise.

She blinked away the tears stinging her eyes, and as she watched Matt and Holly walk toward her, she clamped down on the urge to run to them. They stopped in front of her, and as she looked into his eyes she saw something flicker in their blue depths, a look that sent her heart into a tailspin.

'Hello, Autumn,' he said softly.

'Hello,' she answered.

'See, Mummy, I told you he would come,' Holly said, triumphantly.

'Yes, you did,' she answered, her eyes still on Matt.

'I tried to call you from the Toronto airport, but I couldn't get through. The operator said the circuits were all busy,' Matt explained. 'I gave up when they called my flight. I made it just in time.'

Holly nodded, her eyes shining with love.

'Darling, there's your teacher. You'd better get ready,' Autumn prompted.

'Off you go,' Matt said. 'We'll go in

and find a good seat.'

'Okay,' Holly said, and went with her instructor to the dressing room.

Autumn and Matt followed. Once inside, Autumn turned to Matt. He was staring intently at her now, and her heart skipped crazily for a second. 'I . . . now that you're here, it isn't really necessary for me to stay,' she said.

He glanced around at the small crowd making for the stands. 'It looks to me like quite a few moms have shown up. Surely they won't throw you out if you stay?'

'No, I don't suppose they will,' she said, unable to stop the smile his words elicited.

'Then stay,' Matt said, his eyes holding hers for several seconds. Taking her silence as agreement, Matt put his hand on her elbow and directed her toward two vacant front-row seats.

As they filed past some spectators, Autumn smiled and nodded at the faces she recognized, but all the while she was aware of only Matt beside her.

Even through the thickness of her wool coat, she could feel a warmth spread through her at his touch.

Not until she was seated did Autumn realize Matt was no longer using crutches. 'Your knee must be better,' she commented.

'It's improving, yes,' Matt replied.

Someone tapped her on the shoulder, and Autumn turned to acknowledge a greeting. It was several minutes before she turned back to Matt. He was talking to the man sitting next to him.

There was no opportunity for further conversation between them as the lights dimmed and Miss Audrey, the skating instructor, appeared at center ice. She waited for the applause to die down before she spoke.

Autumn remembered only snippets of the hour and a half that followed. Though her eyes were on the ice, her thoughts were on the man seated next to her. There was something different about him tonight. She'd sensed it the moment her eyes met his. He had about him an air of excitement, reminding her of the way Holly had been all day.

When at last Holly's class skated onto the ice, Autumn felt pride swell in her throat. Her eyes filled with tears, and when she glanced at Matt, the look of love she saw in his eyes took her breath away.

It's for Holly, not me. She shouted the urgent warning to her heart, fighting the emotion threatening to overwhelm her.

It took every ounce of strength she possessed to drag her eyes away from his, and for the half hour that remained of the program she was unaware of anything around her.

When the small but appreciative audience broke into applause, signifying the end of the evening, she heaved a sigh of relief. They rose and joined the group of happy and proud parents chatting and shaking hands. As Matt led Autumn back to the main area, she saw Linc talking to someone near the dressing rooms, but other than raising his hand in acknowledgement, he made no move toward her.

The door to one of the dressing rooms opened and out spilled a group of children, their faces pink with effort and their smiles wide.

'Here she is,' Matt said, spotting Holly first. He smiled and waved to attract her attention, and Holly came running toward them.

The journey home was completed amid a combination of laughter and excited chatter. Holly never stopped talking for more than a minute, and Autumn, driving through the darkened streets, was content to simply listen to their conversation.

She parked the car, and with Holly holding on tightly to her hand on one side and Matt's on the other, they entered the house.

'I'm thirsty. Can I have a glass of pop? Please?'

'All right,' Autumn agreed as she helped Holly off with her jacket.

'Can I have some cookies, too?'

'Tell Mrs. Brady I said you could have a whole plate of cookies,' Matt said. 'You were wonderful tonight, and I bet one day you'll make a terrific figure skater.'

'You really think so, Uncle Matt?' Holly's smile couldn't get any wider.

'You betcha,' he said.

Holly laughed and ran to the kitchen. She stopped in the doorway. 'Aren't you coming, too?' she asked.

'We'll be there in a minute. I need to talk to your mother. We'll be in the living room if you need us.'

'Okay,' Holly said, and disappeared into the kitchen.

Autumn's pulse leaped in alarm at Matt's words. But before she could say anything Matt ushered her into the living room. He closed the door quietly and turned to her.

'Matt, I don't think — '

The words died in her throat as he pulled her into his arms and brought his lips unerringly down on hers.

For timeless seconds she simply

floated in that wondrous world of awakening passion. The heat coursing through her had everything to do with this man and the fact that she loved him heart and soul. She could scarcely believe he was here and that this was indeed happening to her.

For the first time in days Matt felt totally alive. He loved her! He'd never thought it possible to love anyone as much as he loved Autumn.

And it was because of those feelings that he wanted to marry her. He was sure after the clumsy, asinine way he'd proposed to her that she believed he only wanted to marry her as a means to be close to Holly.

Sometime during the flight from Toronto he'd decided that he had to lay his heart at her feet, tell her his feelings. He no longer cared why she'd married Paul. Their life was here . . . now.

He was convinced that in some small measure, at least, she cared for him. Her body was telling him that, even if her heart wasn't.

Slowly now, with a stop he hadn't known he possessed, he brought them both back from the edge of sanity, banking the fires roaring in his blood. As he drew away he saw the desire still smoldering in the depths of her eyes, and it was almost his undoing.

'I love you.' He spoke the words softly, yet clearly, and with a depth of emotion that made him tremble.

'What . . . what did you say?' She shook her head, trying to clear the remnants of passion still clouding her brain. She couldn't believe what she'd heard. It couldn't be real . . . could it? Had Matt really said he loved her?

Matt bit back a sigh of exasperation. 'I love you! I love you! How many times do I have to say it before you believe me.' He ran a hand through his hair. 'I should have said it five years ago,' he said to himself as he turned away.

'What?' Autumn grabbed his arm, fully alert now, and desperate to have him repeat the words he'd mumbled.

'Dammit, Autumn. I said I love you.'

'No! What did you mumble just now?' She moved to within inches of him, urgency in every line of her body.

Matt frowned. 'That I should have told you that night on the beach, but I was leaving. I didn't think it would be fair to you.'

'So you made the choice for me, is that it?' Autumn stammered, still trying to take in what Matt had said.

'You were in the middle of training to be a nurse. How could I ask you to give that up? You were so young.' His words trailed off as he watched an array of emotions play across her face. But before she could speak he hurried on. 'Those few weeks in Europe were hell. I couldn't get you out of my mind — the way you'd looked when I told you I was leaving.' He closed his eyes for a moment at the memory. 'By the time I'd decided to call you,' he went on, 'I remembered you'd told me you were moving. I called Paul instead, but there was no answer. I kept trying, but it wasn't until the day we were on our way to Prague that I finally got hold of him. Our bus stopped at the border, and while we waited to cross I decided to try again. This time I got through, and I asked Paul to pass on a message to you — '

'A message?' Autumn cut in, her heart skipping crazily at the thought that Matt had had second thoughts.

'I didn't have much time. I asked him to tell you I was sorry and that I'd get in touch with you when I got back from Europe. Then the guys started yelling at me to get back on the bus . . . '

'But Paul didn't say . . . I mean I never . . . ' Autumn's voice died to a whisper and tears filled her eyes.

'Paul didn't tell you?' Matt knew the answer even before he asked the question. 'My God.' His thoughts raced on. 'If you didn't get my message, then you must have thought — ' Rage coursed through him as he realized Paul must have deliberately omitted to pass his message on to Autumn.

But why? Matt's thoughts flitted back

to that summer five years ago, remembering now that when he'd begun to date Autumn he'd spent less and less time with Paul. Autumn had been Paul's friend, and perhaps he'd felt a little jealous or resentful of their relationship. Paul had been quiet and at times sullen, but Matt had put it down to artistic temperament, assuming that his brother's moodiness stemmed from the fact that the new painting he'd been working on hadn't been going well.

But on reflection Matt saw now that Paul's behavior had been reminiscent of the way he'd acted when his mother married Matt's father. Paul had resented the fact that he'd had to take second place in his mother's affections, and at times Matt had been the one on whom he'd vented his hostility and jealousy.

Matt cursed under his breath, angry at himself now for not seeing the signs. He'd been wrapped up in his own world, too busy falling in love with Autumn to pay close attention to Paul.

He saw now with a flash of insight that by ignoring Paul he'd undoubtedly contributed to the resurgence of his brother's hostility and jealousy.

Matt faced Autumn once more, seeing the pale features and the look of shock in her eyes. 'As far as you were concerned, I'd vanished,' he said.

'Yes, and as the weeks went by — ' She broke off; the memory was too painful.

'Did you try to track me down?' Suddenly he needed to know.

She nodded. 'I called the team office in Toronto to ask for your number, but they wouldn't give it out. I should have left a message, but I kept hoping.' She swallowed. 'Then I ran into Paul.'

'What did he tell you?' Matt said urgently.

Autumn blinked. 'He said that doing a disappearing act was a trick of yours, then he said he'd get a message to you.'

White-hot rage kept Matt speechless for a moment. Nothing he could do would change what had happened.

Nothing he could say would undo the pain they had both suffered at Paul's hands.

'I never received it, just as you never received mine,' Matt said, shaking his head, unable to believe the depth of Paul's deception.

There remained only one question that needed to be answered. 'But what I don't understand is why you married him.'

Matt's gaze held hers for a long moment, and she knew that the time for evasion was over. Paul had done enough damage. Matt deserved to know the whole truth. It was time to put the past to rest.

Autumn drew a deep breath. 'You'd gone, and when I found out I was pregnant, I had nowhere to go and no one to turn to. I ran into Paul at the hospital, and I suppose we were both in need of a friend.'

'Do you mean he was sick even then?' Matt asked, hearing the inference in Autumn's words.

'Yes. He'd only just found out.'

'My God!' Compassion suddenly replaced his anger as Matt tried to imagine the turmoil Paul must have been going through. 'But I still don't see — ' He broke off. He had no right to ask.

'It was several weeks before he proposed,' she went on. 'At first I was shocked, but he was very persuasive. I had a child to think about, and he was in a position to help me financially. It was to be a marriage of . . . convenience.' She got the word out, but avoided looking directly at Matt. 'I didn't have a lot of choices,' she continued. 'I couldn't continue at nursing school, and the chances of finding a job . . . Paul knew I desperately wanted to keep the baby and he offered me a way to do just that. And in return he wanted me to take care of him. Fair exchange, he said.'

'So you accepted.' Matt's tone held no trace of either accusation or condemnation concerning the decision she'd been forced to make.

Her glance slowly lifted to meet his, and when she saw understanding in his eyes, tears formed in hers.

Matt was instantly at her side. 'Don't! Please don't cry,' he implored her.

Bravely Autumn fought back the tears, but one lonely teardrop spilled over and trickled slowly down her cheek. Matt gently touched a finger to the wetness, and her heart stopped.

'Why did you want to keep the baby, Autumn?' His question brought tears to her eyes once more.

Her heart thudded against her chest as she took a deep breath, trying to stop the trembling threatening to take control. 'Because she was all I had left of you.' Her voice was a harsh whisper of pain.

It was a long moment before Matt could speak. 'Are you saying what I hope you're saying?'

Her smile was a little tremulous. 'Yes! I love you, Matt. I've always loved you.'

Her words were instantly buried under the urgent demands of his lips, soon they were lost in a world of their own making.

It was some time before Matt had the strength or the inclination to talk again. He held her to him, waiting for the need racing through him to ease.

'Paul has put us both through a kind of living hell, hasn't he?' Matt spoke the words softly, as he pulled Autumn down with him onto the love seat. 'But I suppose he must have been living in a horrible kind of hell of his own.'

'Yes ... he was,' she answered, moved by the compassion and forgiveness she could hear in his voice.

They were silent for a long moment. Then Matt eased Autumn away from him. There was a hint a humor in his eyes now. 'Can I safely assume that your answer to my proposal is yes?'

For a moment she pretended to think carefully, and was immediately kissed roughly for her impertinence. 'Yes! Yes!' she almost shouted when at last he released her. 'Holly and I have never been to Toronto. I'm not sure we'll like it.' Her tone was teasing, knowing all too well that if he lived on the moon, she would gladly go there with him.

'Who said anything about moving to Toronto?' It was Matt's turn to tease now.

Autumn pushed against his chest with her hands, but Matt held her with little effort. 'You play for their hockey team. Or have you been fired?'

He laughed, the sound like music to her ears. 'Fired! Good heavens, no. I quit!'

'Quit?'

'There will be an official statement in the morning. You're looking at the new coach of the minor league team known as the Vancouver Devils.'

Autumn could only stare in utter amazement. 'But how? When?'

'Do you remember the man who came into the hospital room and interrupted us?'

Autumn felt a blush tinge her cheeks. 'Yes.'

'That was the second time I'd run into him. The first time was when I dropped Holly off at her skating lesson. Stan Kirkwood is his name, and at one time he was quite a star hockey player himself. I've known him for a number of years and admired him a great deal. He asked me if I'd ever thought about coaching in the minor leagues. He said he was ready to retire, and if I wanted the job it was mine.' Matt squeezed Autumn's hand gently before continuing. 'I thought he was joking, but when he came to my room at the clinic and repeated the offer, I knew he was serious. He was visiting one of his players who was in for treatment, and I never did find out how he knew I was there. Anyway, he sat and talked for about two hours and convinced me I was the man he wanted.'

'But I thought you said your knee was fine?'

'It is. David assured me there was no reason why I couldn't take up where I left off. But for the first time in my life

I wasn't sure I really wanted to go back. Finding out about Holly, falling in love with you all over again . . . ' He stopped to drop a kiss on her lips. 'My priorities changed, and suddenly I found myself thinking that maybe it was time I took a look at where I was going and what I was doing. I've had good innings. Hell!' He laughed. 'I've had great innings. And as Stan said, maybe I can help someone else fulfill their dream.'

'Matt, that's wonderful.' She leaned over and kissed him.

'What's wonderful?' Holly asked suddenly from the doorway. 'And why did you kiss Uncle Matt, Mummy?'

'Because he's a pretty special guy,' Autumn said, holding out her hand to their child, still barely able to believe Matt was here, that this was happening.

Holly crossed the room, and Autumn lifted her onto the love seat.

A puzzled frown creased Holly's face as she snuggled happily between them. 'Maybe one day he could be my new daddy,' she said, her tone more than a little hopeful.

Over Holly's head Autumn gazed longingly into Matt's eyes.

'I think something could be arranged,' Matt said, his tone serious, and there was no mistaking the love shining in the depths of his eyes.

'Promise?' Holly asked.

Matt leaned over and gently captured Autumn's mouth with his own in a kiss that was brief yet totally devastating. 'Promise,' he said, and Autumn knew without a shadow of a doubt that Matt would fulfill this promise and many, many more.

THE END

We do hope that you have enjoyed reading this large print book.

Did you know that all of our titles are available for purchase?

We publish a wide range of high quality large print books including:
Romances, Mysteries, Classics
General Fiction
Non Fiction and Westerns

Special interest titles available in large print are:
The Little Oxford Dictionary
Music Book, Song Book
Hymn Book, Service Book

Also available from us courtesy of Oxford University Press:
Young Readers' Dictionary
(large print edition)
Young Readers' Thesaurus
(large print edition)

For further information or a free brochure, please contact us at:
Ulverscroft Large Print Books Ltd.,
The Green, Bradgate Road, Anstey,
Leicester, LE7 7FU, England.
Tel: (00 44) **0116 236 4325**
Fax: (00 44) **0116 234 0205**

CYPRUS DREAM

Sheila Holroyd

Lorna had come to Cyprus reluctantly, as her aunt's holiday companion. There she met James, who helped her to find out that there was more to the island than hotels and beaches. But could he save her when a ruthless scheme to exploit the island's beauty put her in deadly danger? What would happen to their growing friendship when the holiday was over? And what were her aunt's secret plans?